I0822609

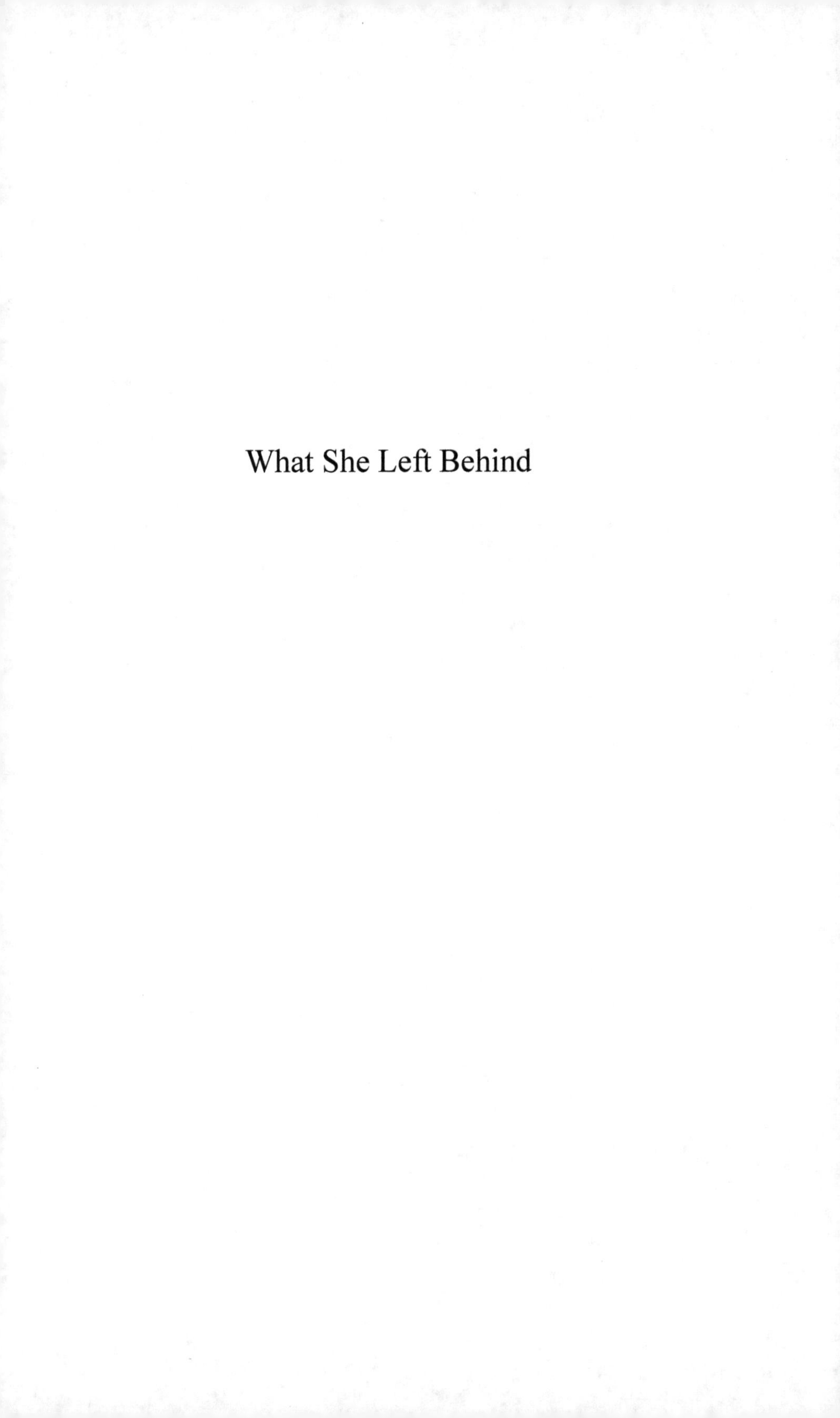

What She Left Behind

What She *left behind*

a novel

Trae Spears

Spears Publishing

Spears Publishing

This is a work of fiction. Names, characters, places, and incidents are products of the author's imagination or are used fictitiously and are not to be construed as real. Any resemblance to actual events, locales, organizations, or persons, living or dead, is entirely coincidental.

Originally published in the United States in 2025 by Spears Publishing.

ISBN: 978-1-959816-12-6

For my family and friends.
Thank you for always supporting
my dreams.

Because in the end, the only thing that really matters… is love.

Messy, stubborn, perfectly imperfect love.

That's what lasts.
That's what we keep.
That's what we pass on.

-Trae

1

The Executor

-Jolene-

Present Day - Thursday, 10:00 am

I've been dreading this drive for two weeks.

The GPS tells me I have fifteen minutes left until I reach Mama's house—*my* house now, technically, though that feels like wearing someone else's clothes. Everything about this feels wrong. The executor paperwork folded in my purse, the spare key Bobby insisted I take from Mama's keychain before the funeral, even the way I'm gripping the steering wheel like it might fly away if I let go.

Bobby offered to come with me. Sweet man sat at our kitchen table in Knoxville, coffee growing cold while I stared at the estate lawyer's checklist for the hundredth time, and said, "Jo, honey, you don't have to do this alone."

But I do. Mama made me the executor for a reason, and if there's one thing I learned growing up as the oldest daughter in our chaotic household, it's that someone has to hold everything together. Might as well be me.

The familiar exit sign for Gulfport appears ahead, and my stomach clenches. I haven't been back since the funeral, and before that, it had been much longer. Mama never made us feel guilty about not visiting enough, but she didn't have to. The guilt lived in my chest like a second heartbeat anyway.

I turn onto Magnolia Street—named long before my sister came along, though Mama always joked that the universe was just preparing for our Nolie's dramatic arrival. The irony isn't lost on me that I'm driving down a street named after the sister who couldn't be bothered to help with any of this mess until now.

That's not fair, and I know it. Magnolia's coming. They're all coming. Merritt, Wren, even little Delilah. We'll sort through Mama's belongings together like some grief-stricken cleaning crew, dividing up a lifetime of memories into neat piles: keep, donate, trash.

The thought makes my chest tight.

I slow down as Mama's house comes into view—the little white cottage with blue shutters that Daddy painted the summer before he got sick. The azaleas are blooming wild and pink along the front porch, exactly the way Mama liked them. "Controlled chaos," she used to say about her gardening philosophy. "Like raising daughters."

I park in the driveway behind Mama's old Buick, which we'll have to deal with eventually, too. Another item for the endless executor's checklist. The car still has her handicap placard hanging from the rearview mirror, and something about that small detail—the evidence of her declining mobility, the admission that she needed help—makes my throat burn.

Bobby called this morning while I was loading my suitcase. "You sure you're ready for this?"

"Ready as anyone can be for sorting through their dead mother's life," I'd said, then immediately felt awful for the sharp edge in my voice. Bobby didn't deserve that. He's been nothing but patient with my grief, even when I've been impossible to live with these past few weeks.

"I just mean," he'd said gently, "it's going to be hard. All those memories in one place."

He was right, of course. Bobby's always right about the emotional stuff. It's one of the things I love about him—he sees feelings coming like storm clouds on the horizon and knows enough to batten down the hatches. But he didn't grow up in this house. He doesn't know what it's like to have every corner holding a story, every drawer hiding some piece of your childhood.

I sit in the car for another minute, air conditioning humming, gathering courage. Through the windshield, I can see the front porch where Mama used to sit with her sweet tea every evening, waving at neighbors and calling out commentary on their yard work. The porch swing Daddy built still hangs there, slightly crooked because he was better with numbers than carpentry.

My phone buzzes. A text from Merritt: *Almost there. How's it looking?*

I type back quickly: *Like Mama. Beautiful and overwhelming.*

Another buzz, this time from Wren: *Delayed at airport but should be there by dinner. Delilah's excited to see everyone.*

And then, because the universe has a sense of humor: *Flight lands at noon. Prepared for emotional devastation. - Magnolia*

Only Nolie would sign her texts like formal correspondence while simultaneously making jokes about family trauma.

I take a deep breath and turn off the car. The silence hits immediately—no more engine noise, no more air conditioning, just the thick Mississippi heat and the sound of cicadas starting their afternoon chorus. Even the air smells like memory here: magnolia blossoms and pine trees and something indefinably *home* that I can never quite replicate in Tennessee.

The front door key turns easily—Mama never did believe in changing locks—and then I'm standing in her living room, surrounded by the accumulated evidence of eighty-three years of living.

"Sweet Jesus," I whisper to no one.

I knew it would be bad. Mama was never what you'd call a minimalist. But seeing it all now, without her bustling presence to make sense of the chaos, it's overwhelming. Boxes everywhere, labeled in her spidery handwriting: "Christmas ornaments - handle with care," "Daddy's Army papers," "Girls' baby clothes - too precious to toss."

The furniture looks smaller somehow, like it's been holding its breath since she died. Her chair still has the shape of her body pressed into the cushions, and there's a half-finished crossword puzzle on the side table next to a coffee cup with a lipstick print on the rim. The cup says "World's Greatest Grandma" in purple letters—a gift from Delilah last Christmas.

I should start somewhere logical. Make a plan. Create a system.

Instead, I sink onto her couch and let myself cry for the first time since the funeral.

The tears come hard and fast, the kind of sobbing that feels like it's being pulled from somewhere deep in my chest. I cry for the crossword puzzle she'll never finish, for the lipstick print that feels too intimate to wash away, for the fact that I'm sitting in her house making plans to dismantle her life piece by piece.

Mostly, I cry because I'm tired. Tired of being the one who handles things. Tired of the endless phone calls with lawyers and insurance companies. Tired of pretending I know what I'm doing when the truth is I feel like I'm drowning in paperwork and decisions and the weight of everyone else's expectations.

When Bobby and I got married twelve years ago, I thought I'd finally found someone to share the load with. And he does, in his own way. He handles our finances, keeps our house running, never complains when I work late or stress-cook my way through a crisis. But this—my family, our complicated history, the way we love each other and drive each other crazy in equal measure—this is still mine to carry.

The sound of gravel in the driveway makes me sit up and wipe my eyes. Through the front window, I can see Merritt's little Honda pulling in behind my car. She's early, which is so perfectly Merritt—always punctual, always trying to help without being asked.

I stand up and smooth my hair, checking my reflection in Mama's hallway mirror. My eyes are red, but there's nothing to be done about that now. At least my mascara is waterproof.

I quickly open the front door—family tradition; we don't wait for a knock—and Merritt steps inside carrying a small suitcase and what looks like a casserole dish.

"You're early," I say, and my voice sounds almost normal.

"You sound surprised," she replies, setting down her things and looking around the room with the same expression I probably had. "Oh, Jo. This is..."

"I know."

We look at each other for a moment, two sisters standing in our childhood home, surrounded by the remnants of our mother's life. Then Merritt crosses the room and hugs me, hard and sudden and exactly what I needed.

"I brought tuna casserole," she says into my shoulder. "Figured we'd need comfort food."

"Did you make it yourself, or did you buy it and put it in one of your dishes?"

"Store-bought," she admits. "But I transferred it to a nice dish, so it counts as effort."

I laugh despite everything. "Mama would approve of the dish transfer. She always said presentation matters."

"Even for grief food."

"Especially for grief food."

We separate, and Merritt looks around the room again, taking inventory. She's always been the practical one, quieter than the rest of us, but steady in a way that makes you feel grounded just being near her. Where Magnolia burns bright and Wren nurtures everyone, Merritt observes and plans and somehow always knows exactly what needs doing.

"Where do we start?" she asks.

"I have no idea," I admit. "I've been sitting here for twenty minutes trying to figure that out."

"Well," she says, hanging her purse on the back of Mama's chair, "good thing you don't have to figure it out alone."

And for the first time since I pulled into the driveway, I believe that might actually be true.

2

Opal Mae

Six Months Ago

The silence is the hardest part.

Not the empty bed, though that's terrible enough—forty-seven years of marriage and my body still reaches for Melvin every morning, finding only cold sheets and the ghost of his Old Spice cologne. Not the meals for one, though I keep making enough cornbread for four people out of pure habit. Not even the way his spot on the sofa sits empty every evening, still shaped to his body like a shrine I can't bear to disturb.

It's the silence that's killing me.

Melvin was a quiet man, never one for unnecessary chatter, but he filled the spaces between words with his presence. The rustle of his newspaper. The soft grunt when he stood up too fast. The way he'd hum old hymns under his breath while tinkering with something in the garage. For forty-seven years, this house has had a soundtrack, and now it's gone quiet as a tomb.

I'm sitting in my kitchen at 2:47 in the morning—I know because I've been watching the microwave clock like it might tell me the secret to sleeping without him—and the refrigerator hums, and somewhere a board creaks, and that's it. That's the whole symphony of my life now.

The girls don't understand why I won't move to one of those senior communities. Jolene's been sending me brochures for months, glossy things full of smiling old people playing cards and doing water aerobics. "Mama," she says every time she calls, "you shouldn't be rattling around in that big house all by yourself."

But this isn't rattling. This is remembering.

Every corner of this house holds us. The kitchen window where I watched Melvin teach Magnolia to ride her bike in the driveway, running alongside her with his hand on the seat until she was flying free. The living room where we spread blankets on Christmas morning while the girls tore through presents like tiny hurricanes. The front porch where we sat every evening for forty-seven years, watching the neighborhood change and our daughters grow up and move away.

I can't leave the memories. They're all I have left of him.

The lawyers keep calling about the will. "Mrs. Calloway," they say in their polite, professional voices, "it's important to have these documents updated." As if I don't know my own mortality is staring me in the face. As if losing Melvin wasn't a reminder enough that none of us are promised tomorrow.

But how do you divide a lifetime? How do you decide which daughter gets the house where they all learned to walk, to fight, to forgive? How do you choose who inherits the place that made them who they are?

Jolene assumes it'll be her, of course. She's the oldest, the responsible one, the executor. She's been handling my affairs since Melvin got sick, driving down from Knoxville every few weeks with her color-coded folders and her gentle but firm suggestions about my finances. Sweet girl thinks love is measured in duty, that devotion means never asking for help.

She gets that from me, I suppose. The need to hold everything together, even when your hands are shaking.

But watching Jo these past few months, seeing how she's thrown herself into caregiving like it's penance for something, I wonder if giving her this house would be a gift or a burden. Another responsibility to shoulder, another way to avoid dealing with her own life.

Magnolia calls from whatever city she's landed in this month—last I heard it was Denver, or maybe it was Phoenix, they all blur together in her whirlwind existence. "Mama," she says, and I can hear the guilt and love and restlessness all tangled up in her voice, "I should come home. I should be there."

"Baby," I tell her, "you're exactly where you need to be."

It's true, though it breaks my heart a little every time. Nolie's been running since the day we buried her daddy, like she could outpace the grief if she just kept moving fast enough. She needs space to figure out that home isn't a place you escape from—it's the place that calls you back when you're ready.

Merritt comes by every few weeks, quiet and steady as always. She brings groceries and checks my smoke detector batteries and sits with me while we watch old movies. She never asks for anything, never expects anything, just shows up and loves me in that careful way of hers. Like she's still not quite sure she's allowed to claim this family as her own.

Oh, my sweet Merritt. If I could give her anything, it would be the certainty that she belongs here as much as any blood daughter. More, maybe, because she chose us and we chose her, and that kind of love runs deeper than genes.

But it's Wrenlee who worries me most.

My baby girl, my peacemaker, carrying everyone else's burdens like they're her own. She calls every Sunday, regular as clockwork, and we talk about Delilah's school and her teaching job and everything except the fact that she's been playing single mother for nearly eighteen years with no help from that worthless man who gave her a beautiful daughter and nothing else.

"I'm fine, Mama," she always says when I ask how she's really doing. "We're doing great out here."

But I hear the exhaustion in her voice. I see it in her face when she visits, the way she makes sure everyone else is taken care of before she even thinks about herself. Just like I raised her to do, God forgive me.

Wrenlee understands that a house isn't just walls and a roof. It's a foundation. A place where love lives and grows and gets passed down through generations. She'd know what to do with this place, how to fill it with the kind of life it was meant to hold.

I get up from the kitchen table and walk through my quiet house, touching the walls like they might tell me something I don't already know. In the living room, I stop in front of the mantel where our family pictures crowd together in a collection of mismatched frames. Melvin and me on our wedding day, young and hopeful and completely unprepared for how hard and beautiful marriage would be. The girls at various ages—gap-toothed school pictures and prom photos and that terrible family portrait from 1995 where everyone looks constipated because the photographer kept telling us to "say money" instead of cheese.

And there, in the center, the picture from Delilah's tenth birthday party. All of us squeezed together on this very couch, Delilah's face chocolate-covered and radiant, surrounded by the women who love her most in the world. Three generations of stubborn, loving, complicated women who know how to hold each other up when the world gets heavy.

That's when I know.

This house doesn't belong to the daughter who stayed closest or worked hardest or followed the rules best. It belongs to the future. To Delilah and whatever comes after her. To the next generation of love that'll fill these rooms with laughter and arguments and the messy, beautiful business of being family.

Wrenlee will understand. She'll know what to do.

I walk back to the kitchen and pull out my good stationery—the cream-colored paper with the little roses that Melvin gave me for my birthday years ago. I've been saving it for something important, and I suppose this qualifies.

"My dearest girls," I write, and then stop, pen hovering over the paper.

How do you explain a decision that goes against every expectation? How do you tell your daughters that love isn't always about fairness, but about what each person needs to grow?

I try again.

"To my Sweet Wren," I write instead. "You'll know what to do."

Because she will. My Wrenlee has always known how to love people into becoming their best selves. She'll figure out what this house needs to become, how to make it serve the whole family instead of just one person's idea of inheritance.

But, just to make sure, I leave a simple sticky note on the back of the deed. I never could help myself when it came to giving my opinion.

The microwave clock reads 3:23 when I finally seal the envelope and put it in my jewelry box for safekeeping. Tomorrow I'll call the lawyer and make it official. Tonight, I'll sit in Melvin's spot on the sofa and listen to the quiet house settle around me, holding all our memories safe until it's time to pass them on.

"You think I'm doing the right thing?" I whisper to the empty room, and I swear I can feel Melvin's hand on my shoulder, warm and steady as it always was.

Trust your heart, his voice seems to say. *It hasn't steered you wrong yet.*

So I do.

3

Sisters Arrivals

-Merritt-

Present Day - Thursday, 11:00 am

I've always been good at arriving precisely when I'm expected and not a moment sooner. It's a skill I developed early—the adopted child's instinct to be exactly what people need, when they need it, without causing any unnecessary fuss.

Jo's car is already in the driveway when I pull up, which doesn't surprise me. Of course she got here first. Jo probably had a color-coded schedule for this weekend, with arrival times plotted down to the quarter hour. The thought makes me smile despite the heaviness settling in my chest at the sight of Mama's house.

I sit in my Honda for a moment, engine ticking as it cools, and look at the little white cottage that raised me. The azaleas are gorgeous—Mama would be pleased. She always said a house without flowers was like a woman without lipstick: technically functional but missing the point entirely.

The tuna casserole on my passenger seat is still warm, though I'm embarrassed it's store-bought. Mama taught all of us to cook, but I never quite got the knack for it the way the others did. Something about following recipes makes me nervous, like I might mess up the measurements and ruin the whole thing. Better to buy something decent and transfer it to a nice dish. At least I remembered to bring a nice dish.

I gather my suitcase and the casserole and head for the front door, fishing in my purse for the spare key Mama gave me years ago. But the door opens before I can find it—another family tradition. We've never been much for knocking in this house.

Jo stands in the doorway, and I can tell immediately that she's been crying. Her eyes are red-rimmed despite what looks like freshly applied mascara, and there's a tightness around her mouth that means she's holding herself together through sheer willpower.

"You're early," she says, and her voice sounds almost normal.

"You sound surprised," I reply, stepping inside and setting down my things. The familiar smell of the house hits me immediately—lavender potpourri and old wood and something indefinably *Mama*—and for a second, I have to concentrate on breathing evenly.

The living room looks like a tornado hit it. Boxes everywhere, labeled in Mama's distinctive handwriting. Furniture that seems smaller somehow, diminished without her presence to give it life. And covering every surface, the accumulated treasures of eight decades of living.

"Oh, Jo," I manage. "This is..."

"I know."

We look at each other across the chaos, two sisters trying to figure out how to dismantle a lifetime. Then instinct takes over, and I cross the room to hug her. Jo's always been the strong one, the one who holds everyone else together, but right now she feels fragile in my arms.

"I brought tuna casserole," I say into her shoulder, because food is love in our family, even when it comes from the grocery store deli counter.

"Did you make it yourself, or did you buy it and put it in one of your dishes?" Jo asks, and I can hear the smile in her voice.

"Store-bought," I admit. "But I transferred it to a nice dish, so it counts as effort."

She laughs, and some of the tension leaves her shoulders. "Mama would approve of the dish transfer. She always said presentation matters."

"Even for grief food."

"Especially for grief food."

We separate, and I take a proper look around the room. It's overwhelming, but not chaotic—more like an archaeological dig through layers of family history. Christmas ornaments mixed with photo albums, jewelry boxes sitting next to recipe cards, a lifetime of keeping and saving and "this might be useful someday."

"Where do we start?" I ask, though part of me isn't sure I want to know the answer.

"I have no idea," Jo admits, and the honesty in her voice surprises me. Jo always has a plan. "I've been sitting here for twenty minutes trying to figure that out."

"Well," I say, hanging my purse on the back of Mama's chair—the same spot I always put it when I was a kid, "good thing you don't have to figure it out alone."

Jo's face does something complicated, relief and gratitude and something that might be tears all mixed together. Before either of us can get too emotional, though, the sound of gravel in the driveway announces another arrival.

Through the front window, I can see a familiar red convertible that looks like it's been through several adventures since I last saw it. The driver's door flies open with dramatic flair, and out steps our sister like she's making an entrance on a movie set.

"Magnolia," Jo says, but she's smiling as she says it.

Magnolia Rhodes—she kept Daddy's name when she got married and divorced and married and divorced again—has never made a subtle entrance in her life. Today, she's wearing oversized sunglasses despite the fact that it's cloudy, a flowing scarf that probably cost more than my car payment, and an expression that suggests she's bracing herself for battle.

She throws a large duffle bag over her shoulder, slams the car door with unnecessary force, and strides up the front walk like she's claiming territory.

"Well, I'm here!" she announces, bursting through the front door without preamble. "Y'all can stop crying and start judging me now!"

"We weren't crying," I say automatically. "We were... honoring. With sarcasm."

I snort despite myself. Only our family could turn grief into a competitive sport.

Magnolia stops in the middle of the living room and slowly removes her sunglasses, taking in the full scope of the chaos. "Good Lord, Jo!!! It's so dusty in here. Did you bring your vacuum or just your judgment?"

"It's in the car," Jo replies without missing a beat. "Right next to my patience."

"Well, good. I didn't bring any of mine."

This is how it always goes with Magnolia and Jo—they circle each other like cats, all affection and irritation in equal measure. I've spent thirty years watching them love each other and drive each other crazy, and I still can't always tell which is which.

"It's good to see you, Nolie," I say, because someone needs to actually welcome her home. "Did you have a good flight?"

"You know my witch's broom gets great mileage," she says, and I'm relieved to hear the humor in her voice. Sometimes, Magnolia comes home angry, all defensive energy and sharp edges. Today, she just seems tired. "What're we doing?"

"Jo and I were just going through these few boxes, waiting for everyone to arrive," I explain.

"Wren isn't here yet?" Magnolia looks around like she might have missed our sister somewhere in the clutter. "I was really looking forward to one of her famous hugs."

"She called from the airport," Jo says. "They lost one of Delilah's bags, so she was raising three kinds of hell."

Magnolia grins. "Oh, no. That poor airport. You know Wrenlee can go from zero to one hundred in two seconds flat when it comes to our Delilah."

"She would do that for any of us," I point out, and it's true. Wren's protective instincts don't discriminate.

"You're right," Magnolia says, and something shifts in her expression. "She always was my fiercest supporter when the rest of you judged my life choices."

There's an edge to her voice now, the old defensiveness creeping in. Jo's spine straightens in response, and I can feel the familiar dynamic starting to reassert itself. Magnolia pushing, Jo pushing back, both of them protecting old wounds that never quite healed.

"Now, Magnolia," Jo says carefully, "you know we never judged you. We just didn't understand you sometimes."

I brace myself for the explosion, but it doesn't come. Instead, Magnolia just looks tired again.

"Oh, right," she says, but without much heat. "I still have your card on my refrigerator from my third divorce. 'You'll get 'em next time.'"

The absurdity of it hits all three of us at the same time, and we start laughing. Not the polite, careful laughter of people trying to avoid conflict, but the real thing—the helpless giggles of sisters who've known each other too long to pretend they're anything other than ridiculous.

"That is kind of funny," I admit, wiping my eyes.

"Right?" Magnolia plops down on the couch and immediately starts digging through the nearest box. "Hand me one of those boxes. I came here to help."

For the next few minutes, we settle into something that almost feels normal. Jo with her clipboard and organization systems, Magnolia making dramatic pronouncements about every item she encounters, me quietly sorting through the more practical things. It's like we're kids again, cleaning our rooms under Mama's supervision, except Mama isn't here to referee when we inevitably start squabbling.

"Oh, my word," Magnolia says, pulling something out of her box. "Remember these?"

She holds up a pair of well-worn high heels, silver with a small bow on each toe. They're scuffed and dated, but I recognize them immediately.

"She wore those to your high school graduation, didn't she?" Jo asks.

"And every play, concert, and that one unfortunate square dancing fundraiser," Magnolia confirms.

"She used to call them her 'Church-to-Cha-Cha' shoes!" I add, remembering.

"She always said if you're going to stand up straight, you might as well do it in heels!" Magnolia's voice catches slightly on the memory.

"And red lipstick," Jo adds softly.

We sit with that for a moment, all of us probably remembering the same image: Mama getting dressed for church or school events, carefully applying her red lipstick in the hallway mirror, stepping into those heels like she was putting on armor. She wasn't a vain woman, but she believed in making an effort, in showing respect for occasions by dressing the part.

"She was always so beautiful," I say.

"She wasn't always the easiest," Magnolia says, "but she was never dull."

"No," Jo agrees quietly. "She wasn't easy."

Something in Jo's tone makes us all pause. There's a weight to her words that suggests we're approaching deeper waters, the kind of family truths that usually stay buried under politeness and good intentions.

We continue working through boxes for what feels like hours, falling into an easy rhythm. The conversation flows around memories and laughter, and for stretches of time, I almost forget why we're here. Then I'll catch sight of Mama's empty chair or hear the particular silence that comes from her absence, and the grief hits fresh again.

"Have y'all found anything else of note in these boxes?" Jo asks, setting aside a collection of what appears to be every church bulletin from the past decade.

"Well, I found this," I say, pulling out an envelope that's been bothering me since I discovered it twenty minutes ago. It's addressed in Mama's handwriting, and something about it feels important in a way I can't quite explain.

"What is it?" Jo asks.

"It looks like a letter... It's addressed to you, Jo... In Mama's handwriting."

Jo goes very still. "A letter?"

"Just Jo?" Magnolia scoots closer to get a better look. "You sure it's not like an old grocery list? You know she always wrote them on her good stationery."

I check the envelope again, reading carefully. "Nope. It says: 'To Jolene. For when the time comes.'"

Jo takes a deep breath, and I can see something shift in her expression—uncertainty, maybe even fear. "Well, the time's come, hasn't it?"

"Don't just stare at it," Magnolia says impatiently. "Aren't you going to open it?"

"No, Nolie. Not right this second."

"Why not?"

Jo's voice gets tight, defensive. "Because I need a minute. Because it is mine. Because maybe I'm not ready to hear what she saved for me. And because it is addressed to me and is none of your business."

The sharpness in her tone surprises all of us. Jo's usually the diplomat, the one who smooths over conflicts rather than creating them. But there's something about this letter that has her rattled.

"Okay..." I say carefully. "We could just keep sorting. There are still plenty of boxes and emotional landmines to go around."

Magnolia, never one to leave well enough alone, grins up at the ceiling. "Yeah, it's probably just a grocery list for her funeral anyway. She'd be real pissed to know that we had it catered. That was Jo's idea, Mama! Haunt her."

Despite everything, Jo cracks a smile. "Oh, hush now. Having to do this with you is punishment enough."

She gives Magnolia a light, playful nudge, and the tension breaks. I can see Jo carefully tucking the letter into her purse, saving it for later when she can process whatever Mama wanted to tell her in private.

Just then, the front door bursts open, and suddenly the room fills with energy and motion as the distinctive tornado that is Wrenlee Sinclair in protective-mother mode enters.

"Sisters!!!!" she calls out, like she's announcing herself to the world.

Behind her comes Delilah, eighteen and lovely and carrying herself with the particular confidence of a teenager who knows she's deeply loved. She's grown since I saw her last—taller, more self-possessed, but still with those bright eyes that see everything and judge nothing.

Magnolia tosses her box aside and jumps up to grab Wren in a fierce hug. "Wren!!! I'm so happy to see you. Ugh, I have been aching for a Wren hug for so long."

"Well, you've got me for the next few days," Wren says, squeezing back. "I will hand them out like candy at Halloween."

She moves to hug Jo and me next, and I'm reminded again why Wren's hugs are legendary in our family. She doesn't just embrace you—she envelops you, like she's trying to absorb whatever pain you're carrying and transform it into something manageable.

"Well, what about me, Aunt Nolie?!" Delilah demands. "You haven't been aching for my hugs?"

"Of course, baby! Get in here!" Magnolia gives Delilah the kind of hug that lifts her off her feet. "Yep, that was the icing on the cake."

"So, what have you ladies been doing?" Wren asks, surveying the controlled chaos we've created. "Have you found anything scandalous yet?"

"You mean like this?" I hold up somcthing I discovered a few minutes ago—an old Bible that feels suspiciously heavy for its size. I open it to reveal a flask nestled in the hollowed-out pages. “I found Jesus… And he brought juice!”

"Oh, my word," Jo says. "Mama did always say that communion was a personal experience."

"And she loved that experience," Magnolia adds with a grin.

We all dissolve into laughter again, and I'm struck by how easily we fall back into this rhythm. Four sisters and a niece, processing grief through humor and shared memories, turning the overwhelming task of sorting through a lifetime into something that feels almost like a celebration.

"Okay," Wren says, taking charge in her gentle but firm way. "Is there any rhyme or reason to the layout of these boxes, or do we just dive in where we are?"

"Believe it or not," Jo says, "there is absolutely no structure to this at all."

Magnolia jumps up to check Jo's temperature with the back of her hand. "Oh, Jo! Are you feeling alright? No structure?"

"Oh, come on," Jo protests. "I can be just as scattered as the rest of you."

"I'd like to see that," I say, and I mean it. Jo's had to be the organized one for so long, sometimes I wonder if she remembers how to be anything else.

"It's okay, Aunt Jo," Delilah pipes up loyally. "They're just jealous that you are able to actually find structure in things."

"Hey!!" Magnolia and I protest in unison, which makes everyone laugh again.

"Thank you, sweetheart," Jo says to Delilah. "I appreciate having someone on my side."

"Always," Delilah says simply, and the love in her voice makes my chest tight.

We spend the next hour working our way through boxes with varying degrees of success. Delilah suggests we sort things into keep, donate, and trash piles, which sounds logical until we realize that everything has a story, and most stories make it impossible to throw anything away.

Mama's knitting set sparks a brief debate until Wren claims it. A mysterious VHS tape nearly gets tossed until I point out the faint crayon marks covering it—marks I remember making when I was seven years old, desperate to claim something as mine in this house full of people who belonged here by birthright.

"I know exactly what is on it," I tell them when they question my attachment to an unlabeled tape.

"You do?" Magnolia asks.

"Yes. It is the video of my first birthday party after Mama and Daddy adopted me."

The room goes quiet for a moment, and I can feel their attention focus on me in that particular way that still makes me slightly uncomfortable. Not because they're judging—they've never made me feel like an outsider, not really—but because moments like this highlight the gap between their childhood memories and mine.

"Oh, Merr," Wren says softly. "That's special. But... how can you tell?"

I turn the tape over in my hands, running my fingers over the crayon marks that have faded but never disappeared. "See the faint crayon marks all over it? I drew on it because it was the first thing that was all for me, and I wanted to make it special."

Jo leans over to look, and her expression softens. "It definitely does have crayon marks all over it. Good eye, Merr."

I hold it carefully, like the precious artifact it is. This tape represents something I've never been able to fully articulate—proof that I belonged here, that there was a moment when this family claimed me as completely as I'd claimed them.

Looking at it now, surrounded by my sisters in the house where I learned what family really means, I can almost hear the echoes of that long-ago celebration. The laughter, the off-key singing, Daddy's voice saying, "We love you, Merritt. Happy birthday."

The first time anyone had ever said those words to me and meant them.

"I guess that is for you," Jo says gently, and I nod, clutching the tape against my chest.

Some things are too precious to share, too important to explain. This tape is proof that I was chosen, that I was wanted, that love doesn't always come from blood but sometimes from the decision to open your heart to someone who needs a home.

And right now, holding this piece of my history in my hands, I remember exactly why this house will always be home, no matter what happens to the deed or the inheritance or any of the practical details that seem so important to everyone else.

This is where I learned that family isn't about where you come from—it's about where you choose to belong.

4

The Birthday

-Merritt-

1985

I know I'm not supposed to listen at doors, but sometimes it's the only way to figure out what the grown-ups are really thinking.

"She's been with us six months, Melvin," Mama's voice drifts through the crack in the kitchen door. "Don't you think it's time?"

"Time for what, Opal Mae?" Daddy sounds tired. He's been working extra shifts at the plant, and I heard Mama tell Mrs. Henderson from next door that money's been tight since they took me in.

"A real birthday party. A proper celebration."

There's a pause, and I press closer to the door, my bare feet silent on the hallway linoleum. I'm not supposed to be out of bed, but I couldn't sleep. The house makes different sounds at night when you're still learning its rhythms—creaks and sighs that might be settling wood or might be something else entirely.

"Opal, honey," Daddy says gently, "we don't even know when her real birthday is."

"January seventh," Mama says firmly. "That's what we decided, remember? The day she came to us. That's her real birthday now."

My throat gets tight. I do remember January seventh—the day the social worker brought me here with my garbage bag of clothes and my scared-rabbit expression. I'd been in three foster homes before this one, and I'd learned not to unpack too thoroughly, not to get too comfortable, not to think words like "forever" or "family" too loudly in case the universe heard and decided to take it all away.

"She's been through enough disappointments," Daddy says. "What if she doesn't want a party? What if it's too much pressure?"

"Then we'll know," Mama replies. "But what if she does want one? What if she's been waiting her whole life for someone to make a fuss over her?"

I think about the birthday parties I've imagined—the kind I've seen on TV shows and glimpsed through other people's windows. Balloons and cake and people who are happy you were born. It seems like something that happens to other children, the ones who belong somewhere from the beginning.

"You really think she's staying?" Daddy asks, and his voice is so soft I have to strain to hear it.

"I know she is," Mama says with absolute certainty. "That little girl is ours, Melvin. She just doesn't know it yet."

The next morning, Mama sits me down at the kitchen table with a serious expression that makes my stomach flutter with worry. In my experience, serious conversations with grown-ups usually end with someone packing my garbage bag.

"Merritt, honey," she says, pouring herself a cup of coffee and sitting across from me. "How would you feel about having a birthday party?"

I stare at her, trying to read her face for clues about the right answer. "Whose birthday?"

"Yours, baby girl. January seventh. We thought it might be nice to celebrate."

"But that's not my real birthday." The words slip out before I can stop them.

Mama's face goes soft. "Sweetheart, do you remember your real birthday?"

I shake my head. The social worker said I was probably born sometime in the winter, but the records were incomplete. My first few years are a blur of temporary places and temporary people, and nobody bothered to mark the day I came into the world.

"Well then," Mama says, reaching across the table to take my hand, "January seventh it is. The day you came home to us. Seems like a perfectly good day to celebrate to me."

"But what if..." I start, then stop. What if I have to leave before then? What if this is all temporary, like everything else has been? What if they change their minds?

"What if what, honey?"

"What if you don't want me anymore before my birthday comes?"

Mama's eyes fill with tears, but she doesn't look away. "Oh, sweet girl. You're not going anywhere. This is your home now. We're your family. And families celebrate birthdays."

"Even if I'm not really yours?"

"Especially then," Mama says firmly. "Being chosen is even more special than being born into a family. It means we picked you on purpose, because we loved you on purpose."

I think about this for a long moment, turning the idea over in my mind like a smooth stone. Being chosen. Being loved on purpose. It's a concept so foreign and wonderful that I'm afraid to believe it too hard.

"What kind of party?" I finally ask.

"Whatever kind you want," Mama says. "We can invite the girls from your new school, or we can keep it just family. We can have chocolate cake or vanilla, balloons or streamers, or both if you want. It's your day, baby. You get to decide."

The freedom of choice is almost overwhelming. In foster care, you learn to be grateful for whatever you get and not to ask for extras. The idea that I could have preferences, that someone would care about what I actually want, is revolutionary.

"Could we have both kinds of cake?" I ask tentatively.

"Both kinds?"

"Chocolate and vanilla? In case people like different things?"

Mama's smile is so bright it could power the whole house. "Absolutely. What else?"

"Purple balloons?" Purple is my favorite color, though I've never told anyone that before.

"Purple balloons. What else?"

"Could we..." I take a deep breath, gathering courage for the biggest request. "Could we invite Jo and Nolie and Wren? I mean, if they want to come."

The three girls who live here have been kind to me, but careful. Like they're not sure if I'm staying either, so they don't want to get too attached. Jo, who's thirteen and serious about everything, has been teaching me how to braid my hair. Magnolia, who's eleven and wild as kudzu, lets me sit with her while she paints her nails. And Wren, who's only nine but acts like she was born to take care of people, always saves me the good crayons during coloring time.

"Honey," Mama says gently, "they're your sisters now. Of course they'll want to celebrate with you."

Sisters. The word hits me like a physical thing, warm and solid and real. I've never had sisters before. I've never had anyone before, not really.

"Okay," I whisper. "Let's have a party."

The next two weeks pass in a blur of planning and preparation. Mama involves me in every decision, from the flavor of ice cream (strawberry) to the color of the streamers (purple and white). She takes me to the store to pick out party plates and napkins, and I choose ones with balloons on them because they look happy.

Jo helps me write invitation cards for the three girls from school I've been tentatively befriending. She teaches me how to make my handwriting neat and reminds me to include all the important information: date, time, address, and "Please come celebrate with me!"

Magnolia insists on helping decorate, which mostly involves her hanging streamers in dramatic swoops while providing running commentary on everything. "Merritt, you have to make the cake-cutting wish count," she tells me seriously. "Birthday wishes are powerful magic, but only if you really believe."

Wren, practical even at nine, helps me plan party games and makes sure we have enough chairs for everyone. She also appointed herself my personal assistant, following me around asking if I need anything and making sure I drink enough water because "party planning is exhausting."

Daddy's contribution is more subtle but just as important. He sets up a card table in the living room for presents, arranging it just so and covering it with a lace tablecloth that belonged to his mother. When I ask him about it, he just says, "Every birthday girl needs a special place for her gifts."

The morning of January seventh, I wake up before dawn, too excited to sleep. For the first time in my life, this day is about me. Not about where I'm going next or whether I've been good enough to stay, but about celebrating the fact that I exist, that I matter to someone.

Mama lets me help make both cakes—chocolate with chocolate frosting, vanilla with strawberry frosting. I get to crack the eggs and measure the flour, and when I inevitably spill some on the counter, she just laughs and shows me how to clean it up without making it worse.

"Cooking is about love," she tells me as we wait for the cakes to bake. "Not perfection. The love is what makes it taste good."

The party isn't until two o'clock, but by noon I'm dressed in my best outfit—a purple dress that Mama bought special for the occasion—and vibrating with anticipation. The house smells like cake and vanilla frosting, and purple balloons bob from every doorway.

My school friends arrive first: Sarah, who sits next to me in class; Emma, who shares her colored pencils; and Katie, who invited me to play hopscotch at recess and didn't seem to mind that I didn't know all the rules. They're polite and excited, the way kids get at parties, but there's still a little distance there. The distance of not quite knowing how to be friends yet.

But when my sisters pile into the living room—Jo carrying a wrapped present, Magnolia with glitter somehow already in her hair, and Wren clutching a homemade card—something shifts. Suddenly, it feels less like Merritt's party with some school friends and more like a family celebration that happens to include guests.

"Happy birthday!" they chorus, and the sound fills the room with warmth.

We play musical chairs and pin the tail on the donkey. We eat cake with our fingers and get frosting on our faces. Daddy is filming everything on his old camcorder, and Mama flutters around making sure everyone has enough punch.

But the best moment comes when it's time for presents.

The gifts from my school friends are nice—a coloring book from Sarah, a pack of hair ribbons from Emma, and a small stuffed rabbit from Katie. I thank each of them genuinely, because someone thought enough of me to wrap something pretty and write my name on it.

Then it's time for family presents.

Jo gives me a jewelry box with a tiny ballerina that spins when you open it. "Every girl needs a place for her treasures," she says seriously, and I understand that this is her way of saying I belong here, that I'm allowed to have treasures now.

Magnolia's gift is a set of nail polishes in every shade of purple imaginable. "So you can always have your favorite color," she explains, and I realize she's been paying attention to what I like, storing up little details about who I am.

Wren presents me with a handmade photo album with "Merritt's Family" written on the cover in careful nine-year-old handwriting. The first page has a picture of all of us at dinner last week, laughing about something I can't remember. "For all the memories we're going to make," she says shyly.

But it's Mama and Daddy's gift that makes me cry.

It's a small wooden sign for my bedroom door, painted white with purple letters: "Merritt's Room." Underneath, in smaller letters: "Part of the Rhodes Family."

"So there's no question," Daddy says quietly, "about where you belong."

I can't speak around the lump in my throat, so I just hug them both as hard as I can. For the first time in my seven years of life, I understand what home feels like. Not a place you might have to leave, but a place where you're chosen, where you're wanted, where you're loved on purpose.

Later, after the friends have gone home and the dishes are washed and the leftover cake is wrapped in foil, we all pile onto the couch to watch the video Daddy took. The camera seemed to capture everything: Sarah laughing with cake on her chin, Magnolia dramatically posing with streamers, Wren carefully helping me open presents.

But my favorite part is the last one—all of us crowded together on this very couch, my family surrounding me like a protective circle. I'm in the middle, chocolate frosting still smudged on my cheek, holding up my hand with seven fingers extended and grinning like my face might split open from happiness.

"We love you, Merritt," Daddy says as the video stops. "Happy birthday."

And for the first time in my life, when someone says they love me, I believe them completely.

That night, lying in my bed—in my room, in my house, with my family sleeping safely around me—I think about Magnolia's advice about birthday wishes. I'd made my wish when I blew out the candles, but looking back, I realize it had already come true.

I'd wished for this to be real. For this family, this home, this feeling of belonging, to last forever.

And as I drift off to sleep, surrounded by the gentle sounds of a house full of people who chose me, I know that some wishes are powerful enough to reshape the entire world.

5

The Peacemaker

-Wrenlee-

Present Day - Thursday, 4pm

I've always been the one who smooths things over.

It's not a role I chose exactly—more like something I fell into when I was nine years old and realized that if I could make everyone else comfortable, maybe they'd be too busy being happy to notice all the ways I felt like I was drowning. Even now, watching Merritt cradle that VHS tape like it holds the secrets of the universe, my first instinct is to make sure everyone's okay, that the emotional temperature in the room stays manageable.

"That's so special, Merr," I say gently, because it is, and because she needs to hear it. Merritt's always been careful with her emotions, like she's still not entirely sure she's allowed to claim space in this family. Moments like this, when her belonging gets acknowledged and celebrated, matter more than the rest of us probably realize.

"We should keep going," Jo says, reaching for another box with the determined efficiency that means she's feeling overwhelmed and trying to control it through productivity. "There are still plenty of boxes to get through."

She's right, of course. We've barely made a dent in Mama's accumulated treasures, and the longer we sit here, the more the weight of it all presses down on us. But there's something about the way Jo's attacking this task—like it's a problem to be solved rather than a life to be honored—that makes my chest tight with worry.

"Okay, the next thing in this box is..." Jo pulls out something that makes her pause. "Mama's babydoll."

I remember that doll. Mama'd had it since she was a little girl, this porcelain-faced thing with glassy eyes and faded pink dress. It used to sit on her dresser, and she'd tell us stories about tea parties and adventures they'd had together when she was young.

"Trash!" Magnolia declares immediately.

"Trash!" Merritt echoes.

"Trash!" I add, because honestly, that doll was just ugly.

"Aha! Jinx! Y'all owe me a Coke," Magnolia says with the first genuine smile I've seen from her today.

"Y'all really want to trash this?" Jo asks, ever the responsible one. "Why don't we donate it?"

"Uh uh," Merritt shakes her head. "That thing always creeped me out."

"I wouldn't even give that to someone I didn't like," Magnolia adds with a dramatic shudder.

"I just thought it was ugly," I admit, which makes everyone laugh.

"Okay. Trash it is," Jo concedes. "Look at us making decisions together."

"Don't jinx it, Jo!" Magnolia warns.

For a moment, it feels like we might actually get through this without anyone bleeding. We're finding our rhythm, falling back into the easy banter that comes from decades of shared references and inside jokes. This is how we work best—together, supporting each other, turning difficult tasks into something bearable through collective effort.

Then Jo reaches into the box again, and everything changes.

"Sorry! Okay, the last thing is this box is..." She pulls out a small jewelry bag and immediately tries to hide it. "Never mind, that was it. Let's grab the next box."

"Uh uh! What was that?" Magnolia's voice sharpens immediately.

"It was nothing. Don't worry about it."

I can feel the shift in the room like a change in barometric pressure. Whatever Jo's hiding, it's significant enough to make her lie about it, which means it's significant enough to cause problems.

"Come on, Jo," I say carefully. "We all have to be on the same page here."

"Yeah, let us see it," Merritt adds.

"You guys, it's nothing. It's mine anyway."

"Well, if it's nothing, why won't you tell us what it is?" Magnolia's getting that edge in her voice that means trouble.

"Because I don't want to start a fight."

"Oh! So it is something, then?!"

I close my eyes for half a second, trying to find that calm center that's gotten me through all these years of single motherhood and countless family crises. But I can already see where this is heading, and there's nothing I can do to stop it.

"Come on, Jo. Just show us what it is," Merritt says.

"Yeah, now I'm really curious," I add, though part of me wishes I could take the words back.

"FINE!" Jo snaps. "It's Daddy's wedding ring."

The silence that follows is deafening. I can hear Magnolia's sharp intake of breath from across the room, and I feel the sudden tension radiating from my sisters like heat from a fire.

"What?!" we all say at once.

This is bad. This is the kind of moment that splits families apart, the kind of hurt that festers for decades if we don't handle it right. And I can already see from the set of Jo's shoulders and the flash in Magnolia's eyes that we're not going to handle it right.

"I thought that was lost," Magnolia says, her voice getting dangerous. "And what exactly makes you think that it belongs to YOU?!"

"Just leave it alone, Magnolia. Grab another box."

"Jo, you don't get to say that after literally hiding a piece of our Daddy!"

Merritt's voice cuts through the rising tension: "Seriously. Why would you tuck it away like that? What, were you planning to just pocket it?"

I try to intervene before this escalates further. "Okay, okay. Can we just take a breath here?"

But it's too late. The dam has burst, and all the careful politeness we've been maintaining is washing away in a flood of old resentments and newer hurts.

"It was in Mama's box, and she left me in charge," Jo says, her jaw set in that stubborn line I know too well. "It's mine to handle."

"'Handle?'" Magnolia's voice goes up an octave. "Seriously?!"

"Wren, she hid Daddy's ring! Who does that?" Magnolia turns to me like I'm supposed to referee, like I can somehow make this fair when fairness was never really an option.

"I did not hide it," Jo protests. "I just... didn't want to make a big deal out of it."

"Jo, we're standing in our childhood home, going through Mama's life in cardboard boxes," Merritt points out with devastating accuracy. "Everything is a big deal right now."

"Exactly!" Magnolia's getting wound up now, her voice carrying all the hurt and frustration that's been building since she walked through that door. "And that ring - he wore that every day. He never took it off! Not even when he got too thin to keep it on his finger!"

I try one more time to calm things down. "Maybe we should just talk about it calmly before jumping to—"

"Oh, come on, Wren," Magnolia cuts me off, and there's something almost desperate in her voice. "Don't start 'calming down the room.' This isn't one of your kindergarten circles. We're allowed to be mad!"

The words hit me like a slap. I know she doesn't mean to be cruel, but it stings anyway. I've spent my whole life trying to keep everyone together, trying to be the voice of reason when emotions run high, and apparently, it's just seen as me being condescending.

"I'm not saying don't be mad," I say quietly. "I'm saying don't be mean. There is a difference."

But the conversation has already spiraled past the point where logic matters. Jo's face goes tight with hurt and anger, and when she speaks, her voice carries the weight of years of unspoken resentment.

"Well, maybe if someone had stayed long enough to actually grieve with us, they wouldn't feel the need to fight over jewelry right now."

The room goes dead silent. Magnolia's face cycles through shock, hurt, and rage in the space of a heartbeat.

"Oh no," she says, her voice dangerously quiet. "You are NOT doing that."

"Jo—" I start, but she's not done.

"I just needed you here. I needed my sister."

"AND I NEEDED TO BREATHE!" Magnolia explodes. "You think you're the only one who lost him?"

"You both lost him. We all did!" I try desperately to remind them of what should be obvious.

"And we're all still bleeding from it," Merritt adds. "And now we've lost Mama. So, maybe let's stop ripping the stitches out."

But it's too late for reason. The hurt is too big, too old, too deep.

"You know what?" Magnolia says, grabbing her bag. "Keep the ring. Keep all of it. Keep the house, the memories, the guilt. You're the queen of this little kingdom anyway."

"Magnolia, wait—" I call out, but she's already moving.

"He called me his firecracker," she says, and her voice breaks just a little. "I was his. That ring should be mine. But clearly, that's not how things work in this family."

She storms toward the bedroom, and I can hear the door slam from here. The sound echoes through the house like a gunshot.

Merritt follows her, probably to try to talk her down or at least make sure she doesn't do anything too dramatic. That leaves me and Jo sitting in the wreckage of what was supposed to be a healing process.

"This wasn't supposed to happen like this," I say to the empty air.

Delilah appears in the doorway, her face creased with concern. "What in the world is going on? I heard screaming all the way in the shed."

"It's nothing, baby," Jo says automatically.

"No," I say firmly, because Delilah deserves better than lies. "Don't do that to her. Tell her the truth."

Jo gives me a look that could freeze water, then gets up and walks away, leaving me alone with my daughter to explain how love can sometimes look so much like cruelty.

"Mama, what is going on?" Delilah asks, coming to sit beside me on the couch.

I put my arm around her and try to find words for the kind of pain that doesn't have easy explanations. "Baby, we're all just hurting. Your aunts never fully grieved for your pawpaw, and now that your gran is gone, those old wounds are just ripped back open again. They just need some time."

"I wish I could help them," Delilah says, and the earnestness in her voice makes my heart ache. "We're family. Family isn't supposed to fight at times like these. We are supposed to come together and support each other."

"I know, baby. Right now, we just have to love them through it."

But even as I say the words, I'm wondering if love is enough. If there's too much history, too much hurt, too many old wounds that never properly healed. Sometimes families break apart not because they stop loving each other, but because the love gets buried under so much pain that no one can find their way back to it.

I hold my daughter close and listen to the sounds of our family falling apart in the rooms around us—Jo moving things around in the kitchen with unnecessary force, muffled voices from the bedroom where Merritt is probably trying to talk Magnolia off whatever ledge she's climbed onto.

This house has seen so much love over the years, but it's seen its share of heartbreak, too. And right now, sitting in the ruins of what was supposed to be a sacred process of remembering and honoring our mother, I'm not sure which one is going to win.

All I can do is hold my daughter and hope that love really is enough, even when it doesn't feel like it.

6

Watching Over

-Opal Mae-

Present Day - Thursday, 6:30pm

Oh, my girls.

If I could reach through whatever thin veil separates me from that living room right now, I'd knock some sense into every one of their stubborn heads. Here they are, standing in the house where I raised them to love each other, tearing strips off each other's hearts over a piece of jewelry.

Magnolia's in the bedroom now, pacing like a caged wildcat, and I can see Merritt following her with that careful way she has, like she's approaching a wounded animal. My firecracker girl is hurting something fierce, and she's doing what she's always done—turning pain into anger because it's easier to be mad than to be broken.

"That B really pisses me off," Merritt tells Magnolia, and I want to laugh despite everything because even now, my little Merritt can't quite bring herself to say the whole word. Some of that Sunday school upbringing stuck after all.

"Merr, we are adults," Magnolia says firmly. "You can say it. Bitch. That bitch pisses you off."

But sweet Merritt just shakes her head. "Bi... Bit... I can't. Jolene really isn't a B. I really think she means well. She just has a lot on her plate."

"Oh, no. Not you, too. Don't come in here trying to kumbaya me."

If I still had lungs, I'd sigh so deep it would rattle the windows. Magnolia's always been the one who feels everything too much, too hard, too fast. When her daddy died, she couldn't find a way to hold all that grief inside her body, so she ran. And Jo, my practical girl, took it as abandonment instead of desperation.

Neither one of them understands what the other needed. Jo needed someone to stay and help her carry the weight. Magnolia needed space to breathe before the sorrow suffocated her. Both needs were real, both were valid, and both were impossible to meet at the same time.

"Listen, I know you're upset," Merritt says, and bless her heart, she's trying so hard to fix what can't be fixed with words.

"I'm MORE than upset! I'm PISSED. That ring belongs to ME!"

The ring. Lord have mercy, if they only knew. That ring was never about who deserved what or who loved Melvin most. It was about letting go of the need to possess every piece of someone you've lost. But my girls don't understand that yet. They think love is measured in keepsakes and heirlooms, in who gets to claim which memories.

"How much more time do I need to give her?" Magnolia's voice cracks now, and there's the real hurt underneath all that anger. "I mean, it's been 5 years since Daddy died. She has only spoken to me a handful of times until today. Now, it finally comes out that while she doesn't blame me for Daddy's death, she blames me for leaving HER? He was my whole world! I had to get out."

Oh, my sweet, lost girl. She really doesn't know, does she? Doesn't understand that Jo's anger was never about blame—it was about need. When everything was falling apart, Jo reached for her sister and found empty air instead. It wasn't about right or wrong. It was about two hearts breaking in different ways and not knowing how to help each other heal.

Merritt's trying to explain it, bless her: "Because YOU are HER whole world, dummy. Yeah, she had Mama, Wren, and me... But she needed YOU. She needed that firecracker that could turn anything into a joke and make her laugh when she wanted to cry."

And there it is. The truth that took me years to understand about my oldest daughter. Jo carries everyone else's burdens because she thinks that's what love looks like. But what she really needed when her daddy died wasn't someone to help her carry the weight—she needed someone to remind her how to put it down for a little while, how to laugh in the face of sorrow, how to be young and wild and free even when her world was ending.

She needed Magnolia's light to balance her darkness. But Magnolia's light was guttering out, and she had to run to keep it from dying completely.

"All I could think about was getting away from here," Magnolia whispers now, tears finally coming. "I never thought about what I was leaving behind."

In the kitchen, Jo's sitting at my old table, holding that ring box like it might contain the answers to questions she's afraid to ask. She's talking to me like I'm sitting right there with her, which I suppose I am, in whatever way these things work.

"Well, Mama... That went about as well as a squirrel in church." She lets out that dry laugh that means she's trying not to cry. "I tried. I really tried. But every time I look at her—at Nolie—I feel pain inside me again."

Oh, my Jo. My responsible girl, my little mother who grew up too fast because someone had to hold everything together. She's been carrying this hurt for five years now, polishing it like a stone in her pocket, taking it out to examine whenever she needs to remember why she has to stay strong.

"You really did leave a mess here, Mama," she continues. "Not just the boxes and the dust and all the paperwork... but the rest of it. You left me in charge of all of this. You trusted me to handle everything."

If I could, I'd tell her that trust was never about thinking she was the strongest. It was about knowing she was the one who needed to learn that she didn't have to be strong all the time. But some lessons can't be taught—they have to be lived.

"But I'm tired, Mama. I feel like I've been holding my breath since the day you died. Like, if I let myself exhale, everything will fall apart."

The truth she doesn't know yet is that sometimes things need to fall apart before they can be put back together the right way. Sometimes holding your breath just means you forget how to live.

"Everyone thinks I'm the strong one. I've worn that title like a crown for so long I forgot it was made of stone."

Oh, my dear girl. Strength was never supposed to be a burden you carried alone. It was supposed to be something you shared, something that grew when it was given away instead of hoarded.

"And Nolie... she thinks I blame her for Daddy dying. I don't. I never did. I just - When he got sick... when everything was crumbling, and I needed someone to hold onto - she left. She left me."

There it is. The heart of it. Not blame, but abandonment. Not anger, but loneliness. The feeling that when she needed her sister most, Magnolia chose herself instead.

But what Jo doesn't understand yet is that sometimes loving someone means letting them save themselves, even when you need saving too. Magnolia wasn't abandoning her—she was drowning, and people who are drowning can't rescue anyone else.

"I didn't need her to fix it. I just needed her to stay."

The saddest part is that both of them are right. Jo did need Magnolia to stay. And Magnolia did need to go. Sometimes love means impossible choices, and someone always gets hurt.

"I'm trying, Mama. To forgive her. To let it go. But some days... It still hurts."

Forgiveness isn't a destination, baby girl. It's a journey you take one step at a time, and some days you walk backward. But you keep walking anyway, because the alternative is staying lost in the hurt forever.

If I could gather all my girls in my arms right now, I'd tell them what I should have said when I was still breathing: Love isn't about being perfect. It's about being present, even when presence is messy and complicated and painful. It's about showing up for each other, again and again, even when you get it wrong.

The ring doesn't matter. The house doesn't matter. What matters is that they find their way back to each other, that they remember the love underneath all this hurt.

But they'll have to find their own way there. Some bridges can only be built from both sides at once, and my girls are still standing on opposite shores, afraid to take the first step.

All I can do is watch and hope and send them all the love I can manage across whatever distance separates the living from the departed. All I can do is trust that the foundation Melvin and I built in this house—the deep, bedrock certainty that family means forever, even when forever gets complicated—will hold them until they remember how to hold each other.

My sweet, stubborn, beautiful girls. They'll figure it out eventually.

They have to.

7

Jesus Juice

-Magnolia-

Present Day - Friday, 12:30am

I can't sleep.

It's past midnight, and the house is finally quiet after hours of tiptoeing around each other like we're all made of glass. After my dramatic exit earlier—God, I really am Mama's daughter when it comes to theatrical exits—I spent the rest of the evening hiding in the bedroom like a sulking teenager.

Merritt tried to talk to me, bless her heart. She sat on the edge of the bed and said all the right things about Jo meaning well and family being complicated and how we all just need time to process our grief. But sometimes the right things aren't what you need to hear. Sometimes you need someone to say, "Yeah, that was messed up, and you have every right to be mad."

Nobody ever says that to me, though. I'm the dramatic one, the firecracker, the sister who overreacts to everything.

When I get hurt, it's always too much, too loud, too inconvenient for everyone else's comfort.

So here I am at 12:47 AM, sitting on Mama's couch in my pajamas, drinking whiskey out of a coffee mug from the flask I found hidden in that old Bible. If that's not a metaphor for my entire relationship with faith and family, I don't know what is.

The Jesus juice burns going down—cheap whiskey that Mama probably bought years ago and forgot about. But it's warm and familiar and exactly what I need right now. Sometimes you need something stronger than chamomile tea to wash down the taste of family dysfunction.

I'm so lost in my own misery that I don't hear footsteps in the hallway until Jo appears in the living room doorway like a ghost in a bathrobe.

"Couldn't sleep?" she asks.

"No... You?"

She sits down on the couch next to me, careful to leave space between us like we're two animals who haven't decided yet if we're going to fight or flee. The silence stretches out, heavy with all the things we said earlier and all the things we didn't say.

"You know I love you, don't you?" I finally ask, because someone has to start somewhere, and it might as well be with the truth.

"I do. And I love you, too."

We continue sitting in that careful quiet, two sisters who know exactly how to hurt each other and are trying very hard not to do it again. The clock on the mantel ticks steadily, marking time we can't get back.

"Isn't that coffee going to keep you up?" Jo asks, eyeing my mug.

I pull the flask from beside me and hold it up. "It's Jesus juice. Want some?"

Jo reaches into a nearby box and pulls out one of Mama's good wine glasses—crystal that only came out for special occasions. "Fancy," she says with the first real smile I've seen from her all day.

"Only the best for family reconciliation," I say, pouring her a generous portion.

We both take a sip, and Jo makes a face that suggests Mama's taste in whiskey was about as refined as her taste in reality TV. But she doesn't complain, because this isn't about the quality of the alcohol. It's about the ritual of sharing something, of sitting together in the dark and trying to find our way back to each other.

"I'm sorry," Jo says suddenly, the words tumbling out like she's been holding them back for hours.

"Me too," I say, because I am. Sorry for running away five years ago, sorry for not calling more, sorry for letting my own pain become a weapon I used against the people who love me most.

"You have nothing to be sorry about," Jo continues. "I was the one being selfish."

But that's not true, and we both know it. I've been selfish too, in my own way. Selfish with my grief, with my need for space, with my assumption that everyone else would just wait around for me to figure out how to come home.

"You're right. Go on," I say, because Jo needs to say whatever she's been carrying around, and I need to hear it.

"I was just being nice. I know you called me the B word."

"That was Merr. I just told her she was allowed to say bitch."

"Really? With the Jesus juice in your hand?"

I glance down at the flask and grin. "He knows. We're good."

That makes Jo laugh—really laugh, not the careful, polite sound she's been making all day. And something loosens in my chest, like a knot I didn't know I was carrying finally coming undone.

"I really am sorry for making you feel like I blamed you for Daddy's death all these years," Jo says, her voice getting serious again. "That was never the case. I just needed you and couldn't understand why you had to leave the way you did."

There it is. The heart of it. Not blame, but hurt. Not anger, but abandonment. The feeling that when she needed me most, I chose myself instead.

"Why didn't you just tell me, Jo? We're sisters. I can't promise that I would've stayed—I had to get out. But I could've promised to Facetime you every night. I could've promised to call. I could've still been there for you without *being* there for you."

It's the truth I've been carrying around for five years—the knowledge that I could have handled it differently, could have found a way to save myself without cutting everyone else loose in the process. But I was drowning in grief, and all I could think about was escape.

"I don't know," Jo admits. "Everything just happened so quickly. Mama was a mess. Merritt wouldn't speak. Wren was trying to comfort Delilah. And I was just there to handle everything else. By myself."

By herself. That's what I left her with—the weight of keeping everyone else afloat while I ran away to lick my wounds in private. No wonder she's been angry with me all these years.

"You've got to learn to ask for help, sister."

"I just don't want to be a burden to anyone."

"Well, keeping it all bottled up until you explode isn't helping anyone, either."

It's something Mama used to say to both of us, actually. Jo, with her need to control everything, me, with my tendency to run when things got too heavy. We're both terrible at asking for what we need, just in opposite ways.

"I know," Jo says quietly.

"I know that we can't make up for the last five years, but we can start trying to work together now. On this mess."

I gesture around at the boxes and chaos that represent our mother's entire life, waiting to be sorted and divided and distributed like some kind of emotional estate sale.

"This is quite the mess, isn't it?" Jo says.

"Mama never threw anything away. She always said, 'Waste not, want not.' Because who wouldn't want a chipped coffee mug or rice from World War II?"

That makes Jo laugh again, and I feel something settling between us—not forgiveness exactly, but the possibility of it. The recognition that we're both damaged and both trying, and maybe that's enough to start with.

"I want you to have this," Jo says suddenly, pulling something from her robe pocket.

It's the jewelry bag. Daddy's wedding ring, the one we fought over earlier like children squabbling over a toy.

"Jo, are you sure?"

"Well, if you don't want it—"

"No! Give it to me!" I grab the bag quickly, afraid she might change her mind.

When I open it, the gold band catches what little light there is in the room. It's exactly the way I remember it—simple, worn smooth by decades of wear, still holding the shape of my daddy's finger. For a moment, I can almost feel his hand ruffling my hair, hear his voice calling me his firecracker.

"You have no idea how much this means to me," I whisper, fighting back tears.

"I do now. I love you, Nolie."

"Oh, I love you so much, Jo."

We hug then, really hug, not the careful, polite embrace we managed earlier, but the kind of sister hug that says we're going to figure this out, we're going to find our way back to each other, we're going to be okay.

When we separate, I look down at the ring again, this small circle of gold that represents so much more than a piece of jewelry. It's proof that I was loved, that I belonged somewhere, that I was someone's firecracker even when I felt like nothing but ash.

"Thank you," I say, because there aren't really words for what this gesture means. Not just the ring itself, but what it represents—Jo's willingness to let go of her hurt long enough to give me what I need, her recognition that love sometimes means making space for other people's pain.

"I should try to get some sleep," Jo says, standing and smoothing down her robe. "Tomorrow's going to be another long day."

"Yeah, me too."

But after she disappears back down the hallway, I stay on the couch for a while longer, holding Daddy's ring and thinking about forgiveness and family and all the ways we hurt each other trying to love each other.

The house settles around me with familiar creaks and sighs, and for the first time since I walked through that front door, it feels like home again. Not the home I ran away from five years ago, but something new—a place where we can all be broken and still belong, where love is messy and complicated and strong enough to survive our worst mistakes.

I slip the ring onto my thumb—it's too big for my other fingers—and close my eyes. Tomorrow we'll keep sorting through Mama's things, keep figuring out how to be a family without the woman who held us all together. But tonight, sitting in the dark with Daddy's ring on my hand and Jo's forgiveness warm in my chest, I think we might actually make it through this.

We might actually find our way home.

8

The Leaving

-Magnolia-

Five Years Ago - March 2020

The hospital smelled like disinfectant and dying dreams. I'd been sitting in this same plastic chair for three days, watching Daddy's chest rise and fall with mechanical precision, listening to the whisper-soft beep of machines that were doing what his body no longer could.

Jo hadn't left his side except to use the bathroom. She'd set up camp with her color-coded folders and legal pads, turning even this into something she could organize and control. Lists of medications, visiting schedules, insurance forms—as if she could file away the cancer eating through our father's bones.

"You should go home and shower," I said, my voice hoarse from crying and the recycled hospital air. "Get some real sleep."

She looked up from her clipboard, eyes red-rimmed but defiant. "I'm fine."

"You're not fine. None of us are fine. Daddy's dying, Jo."

The words hung between us like a blade. She flinched, then straightened her shoulders in that way she'd done since we were kids—bracing herself to carry whatever weight the world decided to drop on her.

"The doctors said we might have a few more weeks if—"

"Stop." I reached over and pulled the pen from her hand. "Just stop planning for five minutes and look at him."

Daddy looked so small in that bed. When did he get so small? This was the man who used to toss me in the air until I squealed, who taught me to drive in the Walmart parking lot, who called me his firecracker and meant it as the highest compliment. Now his wedding ring hung loose on his finger, and his breathing sounded like tissue paper crumpling.

"I know what he looks like," Jo whispered. "I see it every second of every day."

"Then why are you pretending this is something you can fix?"

She stood up so fast her chair scraped against the linoleum. "Because somebody has to! Somebody has to handle the details and make the decisions and talk to the doctors. Somebody has to—"

"Hold it all together," I finished. "Yeah, I know. That's what you do."

"What else am I supposed to do, Nolie? Fall apart like—" She stopped herself, but not soon enough.

"Like me?" I felt something cold settle in my chest. "Is that what you think I'm doing?"

"I didn't say that."

"You didn't have to." I looked around the sterile room—at the tubes and wires, at the chart hanging from the foot of the bed, at my father disappearing a little more each day. "Maybe falling apart is the appropriate response here. Maybe pretending you can control this is the crazy thing."

Jo's face went white, then red. "Don't you dare. Don't you dare make me the bad guy for trying to—"

"I'm not making you anything. I'm saying maybe grief isn't supposed to look like a filing system."

We stared at each other across Daddy's bed, and I saw something break in her eyes. For just a moment, the perfect mask slipped, and I saw how terrified she was. How exhausted. How desperately she needed someone else to be strong so she could finally let herself crumble.

But I couldn't be that person. Not here. Not like this.

The room felt like it was shrinking, the walls pressing in with every beep of the heart monitor. I needed air. I needed space. I needed to run until my lungs burned and my legs gave out, and I couldn't think about anything except putting one foot in front of the other.

"I have to go," I said, grabbing my purse.

"Where? Visiting hours aren't over for another—"

"I can't breathe in here, Jo. I literally cannot breathe."

"So step outside. Walk around the block. But don't leave. Please." Her voice cracked on the last word. "I need you here."

That's what broke me. Not Daddy dying—I'd been preparing for that since the diagnosis. But Jo needing me, admitting it out loud, and knowing I was going to disappoint her anyway.

"I know you do. But I can't. I can't sit here and watch him die by inches and pretend it's normal. I can't make small talk with nurses and discuss DNR orders and decide what flowers to put on his casket. I can't be who you need me to be right now."

"So you're just going to run away?" The hurt in her voice cut deeper than anger would have.

"I'm going to survive this the only way I know how."

I kissed Daddy's forehead—his skin was paper-thin and fever-warm—and whispered that I loved him. I squeezed Jo's hand, though she didn't squeeze back.

"I'll call," I said.

"No, you won't."

She was right. We both knew it.

I made it to the parking garage before the tears came, ugly choking sobs that doubled me over beside my car. I called in sick to work, drove home, and threw clothes into a suitcase without looking at what I was packing. By sunset, I was on I-10 heading west with no particular destination in mind except away.

Away from the hospital smell and the sound of that damn heart monitor. Away from Jo's disappointed face and her color-coded folders. Away from watching the strongest man I'd ever known waste away to nothing while his daughters argued over medical forms.

I drove for two days straight, stopping only for gas and coffee and to sleep for a few hours in rest stop parking lots. I ended up in New Mexico, in a tiny town where nobody knew my name or my story. I rented a studio apartment above a bakery and got a job waiting tables at a diner where the most complicated decision was whether someone wanted hash browns or grits.

Daddy died on a Tuesday. Jo called me at 6:47 AM Mountain Time, and I knew before I answered what she was going to tell me. Her voice was steady, controlled, like she was reading from one of her lists.

"He's gone, Nolie. This morning, around 6:15. Peaceful. The nurses said it was peaceful."

"Was he alone?"

"No. Mama and I were here. Wren, too—she flew in yesterday. Merritt's on her way."

I wanted to ask if he said anything about me. If he asked where I was. But I was afraid of the answer, so I just said I was sorry and that I'd try to make it back for the funeral.

"Try?" The word came out sharp as broken glass.

"I'm in New Mexico, Jo. It's complicated."

"It's complicated." She repeated it like she was testing how it tasted. "Our father is dead, and you being at his funeral is complicated."

"Don't do this. Please."

"Don't do what? Don't be upset that you weren't here when he died? Don't be hurt that you can't even commit to coming to his funeral? Don't be angry that I've been handling everything alone for two months while you've been off finding yourself in the desert?"

Each word hit like a physical blow. "I didn't want to leave. I had to."

"No, Nolie. You chose to. There's a difference."

The line went quiet except for the sound of her breathing. I could picture her standing in that hospital hallway, still holding it all together even though the person who needed holding together was gone.

"I'll be there," I said finally. "For the funeral. I'll be there."

"Good. Because Mama needs all of us right now, even if she doesn't say it."

After she hung up, I sat on the floor of my little apartment and cried until I had nothing left. Then I called my boss and quit, packed the same suitcase I'd been living out of for two months, and drove back home.

The funeral was everything Jo had probably organized down to the last detail—tasteful flowers, beautiful music, a service that honored Daddy's life without dwelling too much on how it ended. Mama wore her best black dress and accepted condolences with the grace of Southern royalty. Merritt sat quietly in the front pew, holding tissues she didn't use. Wren held Delilah close and whispered comfort to anyone who needed it.

And Jo stood at the back of the church after the service, shaking hands and thanking people for coming, making sure every detail was perfect even though her world had just shattered.

I tried to talk to her at the reception, but she was always busy with something else—refilling the coffee, arranging the casserole dishes, making sure Mama was comfortable. When I finally cornered her in the church kitchen, she looked right through me.

"Thank you for coming," she said, like I was a distant relative instead of her sister.

"Jo, I know you're angry—"

"I'm not angry." She turned back to the coffee pot, measuring grounds with mechanical precision. "I'm tired."

"Can we talk? Really talk?"

"About what? About how you left when I needed you most? About how I sat in that hospital room alone while Daddy asked where his firecracker was? About how I had to plan his funeral by myself because my sister was too busy finding herself to help bury her father?"

Each word was delivered in the same calm tone she used for grocery lists, which somehow made them hurt worse than if she'd screamed.

"I couldn't stay. I tried to explain—"

"You explained. You needed to breathe. You needed space. You needed to survive this your way." She finally looked at me, and her eyes were empty. "Well, congratulations. You survived."

That was five years ago, and we'd barely spoken since. A few awkward phone calls on birthdays. Brief, polite conversations at Christmas when we both called Mama. We were like strangers who happened to share a childhood.

Until now. Until Mama died and left us all in this house together, forced to sort through the pieces of a family that had been broken for half a decade.

Sitting here in Mama's living room, watching Jo organize boxes with the same mechanical precision she'd used for everything since Daddy died, I finally understood what I'd done to her. I'd left her to carry the weight of our family's grief alone. I'd abandoned her when she needed me most, and then I'd had the audacity to be hurt when she couldn't forgive me for it.

Maybe coming home didn't always mean belonging. Maybe some things couldn't be fixed with apologies and good intentions.

But maybe—just maybe—they could be fixed with time and truth and the kind of stubborn love that survived even when everything else fell apart.

9

Lucky Charm

-Merritt-

Present Day - Friday, 1:00am

The house had finally settled into the kind of quiet that felt both peaceful and heavy. Jo and Magnolia's voices had faded from the living room—whether they'd gone to bed or simply run out of words, I couldn't tell. Wrenlee had tucked Delilah in hours ago and retreated to her own room, emotionally wrung out from the day's discoveries.

And here I was, alone in the bedroom that used to be mine, holding the VHS tape that had started it all.

The little television sat on the dresser where it always had, a relic from the days when this room was my sanctuary. I'd brought the tape in here after everyone scattered, needing some space to think, to process everything that had happened. But instead of watching it again, I just sat on the edge of the bed, turning the cassette over in my hands, feeling the weight of all those crayon marks I'd made as a seven-year-old.

"You know, Mama," I said quietly to the empty room, "sometimes I wonder what it would've been like... if I'd been born into this family instead of being brought in like a stray cat someone left on the porch."

The words felt strange spoken aloud, but somehow necessary. Like a confession I'd been carrying for years, finally ready to be heard.

"Not that you or Daddy ever made me feel that way. Not really. You loved loud—you loved us all loud. But there were times... little things."

I could picture them so clearly—all those moments when the others would share memories I couldn't access. Jo talking about her baby blanket, the yellow one with the satin edges that she'd carried everywhere until it fell apart. Magnolia going on and on about how Daddy taught her to ride a bike in the driveway, how he ran alongside her for what felt like hours until she finally found her balance. Wren's first solo in church, her sweet voice filling the sanctuary while Mama cried proud tears in the front pew.

"I'd smile and nod and pretend like I remembered it too," I continued, my voice barely above a whisper. "But I didn't. Because I wasn't there yet."

That was the thing about being adopted at six—old enough to remember another life, another family, but young enough to desperately want to belong to this new one. Old enough to understand that there were years of shared history I'd never be part of, but young enough to believe that maybe, if I tried hard enough, I could catch up.

I sat there holding the VHS tape. The weight of it in my hands felt heavier now, loaded with meaning I'd only begun to understand.

"This... this was the first time I was there. That birthday party."

I closed my eyes and let myself fall back into that memory. Seven years old, wearing that ridiculous purple dress that made me look like a fuzzy eggplant. The fabric had been itchy and the ruffles too much, but I hadn't cared because it was *my* dress, bought specifically for *my* party by the people who had chosen to call me daughter.

"There were streamers and a lopsided cake. But I didn't care. Because for the first time, I wasn't watching someone else's home video... I was *in* it. I was the star of the show."

The memory was so vivid I could almost taste the too-sweet frosting, could hear the slightly off-key rendition of "Happy Birthday" sung by voices that were learning to call me family. But most of all, I could hear Daddy's voice, warm and sure and full of love.

"And Daddy—God, Daddy—he called me his 'lucky charm.' Said I made the family complete."

My throat tightened around the words. Melvin Rhodes had been a man of few words, but when he spoke, every syllable carried weight. He didn't throw around endearments casually or make promises he couldn't keep. So when he called me his lucky charm, when he said I completed their family, it wasn't just nice words meant to make a little girl feel better. It was truth, spoken with the kind of certainty that could anchor a child's entire sense of self.

"*That* stuck with me."

And it had. Through all the years that followed, through every moment when I felt like an outsider looking in, through every family gathering where I smiled and nodded while the others shared memories I couldn't access—I held onto those words like a lifeline.

"Even when I faded into the background. Even when I felt like the understudy in a play I didn't audition for."

I let out a soft laugh, though it came out more rueful than amused. That's exactly what it had felt like sometimes—like I was the backup singer in someone else's song, the supporting character in a story that had been going on long before I arrived.

"Do you know what it's like to be the quiet one in a family this... loud? It's like whispering into a hurricane."

But even as I said it, I realized something. I'd stayed. Through all of it—the chaos and the arguments and the moments when I felt invisible—I'd stayed. Not just physically, but emotionally. I'd planted roots in this family's soil and decided to grow here, even when the weather got rough.

"But still—I stayed. I listened. I laughed at the right moments and cried when no one was watching. I've loved every single one of them with my whole heart... even when it felt like I had to elbow my way into the group hug."

The tears came quietly, without fanfare. Just a slow acknowledgment of all the love I'd carried, all the ways I'd learned to belong to a family that sometimes forgot to make room for the quiet ones.

"I know I'm not the glue. I'm not the firecracker. I'm not the hugger or the fixer or the peacemaker. I'm... me. Just Merritt. The one Mama picked. Daddy's 'lucky charm.'"

And maybe that was enough. Maybe it had always been enough.

"And maybe... just maybe... that means I was meant to be here all along."

I wiped away the tear that had escaped, feeling something shift inside me. Not just acceptance, but something deeper. Recognition. All these years, I'd been waiting for some external validation that I belonged here, some sign that I was as much a part of this family as the others. But the truth was, I'd always belonged. From the moment Mama and Daddy signed those adoption papers, from the first time they called me daughter, from that birthday party when I stopped being a visitor and became part of the story.

"I love them so much it hurts. But if I have to cry about it, I'd at least like to do it with some wine, a blanket, and maybe a cookie. Preferably, one Mama didn't bake. Lord rest her soul, but that woman could burn air."

The laugh that escaped was real this time, full of affection and exasperation and the kind of fond frustration that only comes with deep love. Mama's cooking had been legendary for all the wrong reasons, but we'd eaten every burned casserole and lumpy gravy with gratitude because it was made with love, even if it wasn't made with skill. That’s what she taught us. Not to be a culinary genius, but to put our hearts and souls into everything we did.

I placed the VHS tape on the bedside table, right where I could see it when I woke up tomorrow. A reminder of beginnings, of choosing and being chosen, of the moment when a scared little girl became someone's lucky charm.

"Thanks for choosing me, Mama. I hope I've made you proud."

The room was quiet except for the familiar sounds of the old house settling around me. But in that silence, I could almost hear something else—a whisper of approval, a sense of peace, the feeling of being exactly where I was meant to be.

Tomorrow, there would be more boxes to sort, more memories to navigate, more decisions to make about what to keep and what to let go. But tonight, I was just Merritt. The lucky charm. The one who was chosen and who chose to stay.

And that, I realized, was more than enough. It was everything.

10

The Stranger at the Door

-Jolene-

Present Day - Saturday, 10:30am

I was finally making progress. Real, measurable, clipboard-worthy progress.

The living room had been transformed from yesterday's emotional battlefield into something that actually resembled an organized workspace. Three distinct piles: keep, donate, trash. Color-coded sticky notes marking items that needed family discussion. A master list of tasks broken down by priority and timeline. It wasn't perfect yet, but it was manageable. Controllable.

"Alright, team," I announced, consulting my morning schedule. "Here's today's plan: We tackle the den, the kitchen drawers, and the coat closet. That's it. Manageable, efficient, and most importantly, structured."

Magnolia looked up from the couch where she'd surrounded herself with what appeared to be every piece of costume jewelry Mama had ever owned. She was holding a rhinestone brooch up to the morning light like she was appraising the crown jewels.

"I thought we agreed—no structure," she said with a theatrical yawn.

"We agreed *you* didn't like structure," Wrenlee corrected from her spot by the window. She was folding one of Mama's crocheted afghans with the kind of careful attention that made me wonder if she was thinking about taking up the hobby herself.

Merritt, looking more rested than she had since arriving, lifted her coffee mug in a mock toast. "Don't worry, Nolie. 'Efficient' is code for 'we'll all end up in one room, crying over a single shoelace that reminds us of our childhood trauma.'"

"Like that teacup we found earlier that made you cry!" Delilah added, temporarily abandoning her unnecessary dusting of an already clean side table.

"It had a tiny cat painted inside!" Merritt protested. "Don't judge me."

"It was literally chipped and stained," Magnolia pointed out, though her tone was affectionate rather than critical.

"So am I," Merritt replied without missing a beat. "Your point?"

I smiled despite myself. The easy banter was such a relief after yesterday's emotional explosions. We'd all slept under the same roof and somehow managed not to kill each other. Progress, even if it wasn't the kind I could put on a checklist.

I was just about to suggest we start with the coat closet—tackle the hardest job first, that was my philosophy—when the front door suddenly burst open with enough force to rattle the windows.

A large duffel bag came flying through the entrance like it had been launched from a cannon, followed immediately by a woman who looked like she'd stepped out of a medical drama by way of a music festival. Bright scrubs, neon pink sneakers, hair piled in a messy bun that defied gravity, and sunglasses that were far too large for any reasonable purpose at ten-thirty in the morning.

She moved with the kind of confident energy that suggested she was accustomed to walking into rooms where she didn't belong and making herself indispensable within minutes.

"Hello?" she called out cheerfully, like bursting into strangers' houses was a perfectly normal Saturday morning activity. "Anyone still grieving in here?"

My pen stopped mid-note. Coffee mugs froze halfway to lips. Even Delilah's dusting rag went still. The only sound was the gentle tick of Mama's old mantel clock, marking time in a moment that suddenly felt suspended between normalcy and complete chaos.

"Uh... hello?" I managed, my voice carrying the careful politeness I usually reserved for door-to-door salespeople and telemarketers.

The woman pulled off her sunglasses with a flourish that belonged on a stage, revealing bright, intelligent eyes and a smile that seemed to illuminate the entire room.

"Eliza Staunton. Hospice nurse. Your mama's favorite—not that she played favorites. She told me so herself. 'Eliza,' she said, 'if I had a nickel for every nurse like you, I'd still prefer you.' And then she threw a spoon at me. Miss her like crazy."

The words hit me like ice water. Hospice nurse. The person who'd been with Mama at the end, who'd seen her through those final months when the rest of us were scattered across three states, dealing with our own lives and responsibilities and the complicated logistics of grief.

"Wait—you're Eliza?" Wrenlee stepped forward, recognition dawning in her voice.

"The spoon-throwing story is real?" Delilah asked, momentarily forgetting her manners in favor of curiosity.

"Realer than my last relationship, honey," Eliza replied with a laugh that managed to be both rueful and genuinely amused.

She walked into our living room like she'd been invited, like she belonged here, setting a large Tupperware container on the coffee table with the confidence of someone who knew exactly what she was doing.

My organizational instincts kicked into high gear. Who was this person? How had she gotten in? What did she want? More importantly, how was I supposed to fit an unexpected visitor into the carefully structured day I'd planned?

"I brought muffins," she announced. "They're gluten-free, dairy-free, and taste-free. You're welcome."

Despite everything—the disruption to my schedule, the complete lack of advance notice, the way she'd just walked into our private family moment—I found myself fighting back a smile. There was something about her directness that was oddly comforting.

"Did you say hospice nurse?" Magnolia found her voice first, though it came out slightly higher than usual. "As in, you were with Mama at the end?"

The cheerful mask slipped for just a moment, revealing something deeper underneath. Grief. Real, raw grief that looked remarkably similar to what we'd all been carrying.

"I was. And I cried more than Grey's Anatomy, season eleven, episode twenty-one." She paused, studying each of us in turn with the kind of careful attention that suggested she was used to reading people quickly and accurately. "Who's who?"

Wrenlee stepped into her natural role as family spokesperson. "I'm Wrenlee. This is Magnolia, Merritt, Jolene, and Delilah."

Eliza's gaze moved from sister to sister, and I had the unsettling feeling that she was cataloging not just our names but our personalities, our relationships to each other, our individual ways of carrying grief.

"Hugger," she said, pointing to Wrenlee. "Chaos"—Magnolia raised an eyebrow but didn't protest. "Quiet but judgmental"—Merritt actually smiled at that assessment. "Overachiever"—I looked down at my clipboard and realized she wasn't wrong. "Dust fairy"—Delilah glanced at the rag in her hand and grinned.

"She really was Gran's favorite," Delilah murmured, and something about her easy acceptance of this stranger made me feel like maybe I was being too cautious.

"I don't know whether to be offended or hug you," Magnolia said, though her tone suggested she was leaning toward the latter option.

"Why not both?" Eliza asked, plopping down in Mama's old armchair like she'd been invited to stay for the weekend. "That's how I get most of my friends."

She kicked off her bright pink sneakers without ceremony and immediately pulled out what appeared to be a half-finished scarf and a crochet needle from her duffel bag.

"Are you... crocheting?" I asked, because of all the surprises this morning had brought, watching a stranger whip together a scarf in my dead mother's chair was somehow the most surreal.

"I promised your mama I'd finish this before she haunts me. She said if I didn't, she'd hide my car keys every day for eternity."

"That sounds like her," Merritt said, and there was something in her voice that suggested she was beginning to relax around this unexpected visitor.

Wrenlee sat down across from Eliza, drawn by the same instinct that had always made her our family's emotional compass. "Did she say anything... at the end?"

The question hung in the air like a prayer. We'd all wondered, but none of us had been brave enough to ask. What do you say when you're dying? What wisdom do you leave behind? What final words sum up a life lived fully and messily and with more love than any one person should be able to contain?

Eliza's hands stilled, and for a moment, the cheerful mask dropped completely. What we saw underneath was grief as real and raw as our own, mixed with something that looked like deep, abiding love.

"Oh, girl. She said everything. Gave me her favorite casserole recipe, cursed that love seat"—she gestured toward the tattered white love seat that Mama had bought at a garage sale—" and told me Magnolia still owed her twenty bucks from 2003."

"That's not true!" Magnolia protested with the kind of automatic indignation that suggested this was a long-standing family debate. "I paid her back in candles."

"You gave her two half-burned ones from Bath and Body Works," Delilah pointed out with the precision that only comes from years of family legend-keeping.

"That's practically currency," Magnolia defended, but she was smiling now.

"Oh, and she wanted you all to know—exact words—'Don't fight over my crap. If I wanted you to argue, I'd have hidden the silverware.' Then she winked. I didn't even know she could still wink."

I set down my clipboard, feeling something loosen in my chest. That was Mama, all right. Even dying, she was thinking about us, worrying about us, trying to manage our grief from beyond the grave.

"That woman was a riddle wrapped in a mystery wrapped in a leopard print robe," I said.

"And a wig named Doris," Merritt added.

"She had names for all her wigs," Wrenlee confirmed.

"I loved Peggy," Magnolia said with genuine fondness. "She gave off 'don't mess with me' vibes."

"Pretty sure she was buried in Peggy," Eliza said matter-of-factly. "With a feather boa and a lottery ticket autographed by Madam Mooch."

"The fortune teller?" Delilah asked.

"She's a fraud," Magnolia declared with feeling. "She told me I wasn't Cleopatra in my past life. EVERYONE was Cleopatra—she had multiple personalities."

The laughter that erupted was unexpected but welcome, filling the room with something lighter than the grief that had dominated our conversations. For a moment, it was easy to remember that Mama had been funny and irreverent and completely unique, not just the absence we were learning to navigate.

I watched Eliza's face as we laughed together, and something in her expression suggested she understood exactly what we needed. Not sympathy or professional comfort, but permission to remember joy alongside sorrow. Permission to be human instead of just grieving.

"You know," she said, resuming her scarf, "being around you girls makes me feel like I accidentally wandered into the finale of a family sitcom I didn't know I'd been watching."

"That's not far off," I admitted.

"Except no one's getting a spinoff," Magnolia added.

"I want a spinoff," Delilah declared with the kind of matter-of-fact confidence that made us all smile.

"You're young," Merritt told her. "Give it a few years and a questionable boyfriend."

"In all seriousness, though," Eliza said, her voice taking on a different quality, "she loved y'all. Fiercely. Talked about you like you were made of stardust and fireworks… and bad decisions. But you were hers. Every single piece of you."

The words settled over us like a benediction, and I felt something shift in my chest. Not just about Mama, but about this stranger who wasn't really a stranger anymore. Anyone who could talk about us with that kind of understanding, who could make us laugh while acknowledging our grief, who had clearly loved our mother enough to finish a knitting project under threat of eternal haunting—maybe she wasn't an intrusion after all.

Maybe she was exactly what we needed.

"That sounds like her," Wrenlee said softly.

"She wasn't perfect," I added. "But she was ours."

"Mess and all," Magnolia agreed.

"Mess is just love that exploded a little," Eliza observed, and something about the way she said it suggested she knew exactly what she was talking about.

"That should go on a t-shirt," Merritt said.

"With a cartoon grenade," Delilah added.

"Make it glitter. I'd wear that," Eliza declared.

I found myself reaching for one of her muffins, despite my natural skepticism of anything described as "taste-free." The simple act of eating something—even something that turned out to taste exactly like healthy cardboard—felt like a small step toward normalcy.

"These really do taste like cardboard," I confirmed.

"But healthy cardboard," Eliza pointed out cheerfully.

"Still cardboard," I replied, but I was smiling now.

Suddenly, a loud thump echoed from somewhere deeper in the house, causing all of us to freeze mid-conversation.

"...What was that?" I asked, my organizational instincts immediately shifting into problem-solving mode.

"The ghost of Christmas clutter," Magnolia suggested.

"I vote not opening it," Merritt said firmly. "We've all seen those horror movies."

"I vote immediately opening it," Eliza countered. "Life is short, and I'm nosy."

We all moved cautiously toward the coat closet—the source of the mysterious thump and the bane of my organizational existence for as long as I could remember. I reached for the handle with the careful deliberation of someone defusing a bomb.

When I opened it, a cascade of umbrellas, shoes, and what appeared to be a small accordion tumbled out onto the floor.

"Did Gran play the accordion?" Delilah asked.

"I don't think anyone ever played that accordion," Merritt replied with certainty.

"Should we keep it?" Magnolia wondered.

"One of you play it," I decided. "If it summons a ghost, we trash it."

Eliza grabbed the instrument without hesitation and squeezed out a sound that was somewhere between music and the death rattle of a very large bird.

"I'm either calling a ghost or a goose," she announced, completely unperturbed by the horrible noise.

The laughter that followed was helpless and healing, the kind that comes when grief and exhaustion and the sheer absurdity of life collide in exactly the right way.

"I vote Eliza stays forever," Wrenlee declared when she could finally speak again.

"Agreed," Delilah said immediately.

"All in favor?" Magnolia called out like she was conducting official business.

"Aye!" we all responded in unison.

I looked around at my sisters, at this stranger who had somehow become part of our morning, at the chaos and mess and unexpected joy that had replaced my carefully planned schedule. For the first time since Mama died, I felt something that wasn't just duty or obligation or the crushing weight of being the responsible one.

I felt like maybe, just maybe, we were going to be okay.

"You guys are gonna regret that when I reorganize your spice rack alphabetically," Eliza warned, but her eyes were bright with something that looked like happiness.

"If you can survive Mama, you can survive us," I told her, and meant it.

My clipboard lay forgotten on the coffee table, my carefully structured morning plan completely abandoned. But somehow, with this unexpected addition to our family chaos, the impossible task of sorting through a lifetime of memories felt a little less overwhelming.

Not easy—it would never be easy. But possible.

Because sometimes the best things aren't the ones you plan for. Sometimes they're the ones that burst through your front door wearing neon pink sneakers and carrying terrible muffins and the kind of love that makes everything else seem manageable.

Sometimes they're the people who help you remember how to laugh when you thought you might never laugh again.

11

Finding Family

-Eliza-

1981 - Shreveport, Louisiana

The first thing I ever owned was a plastic hospital bracelet with my name spelled wrong. "Elizibeth Stanton" it read, missing an 'a' and a 'u' that would follow me through three different foster homes before anyone bothered to correct it. I was six months old when they took that bracelet off, replacing it with nothing but a case file and a future full of temporary addresses.

Crystal Staunton—my birth mother—was sixteen when she had me. That's about all I know. Sixteen, scared, and smart enough to know she couldn't give me what I needed. The social workers always made it sound like a gift, her decision to place me for adoption. "She loved you enough to let you go," they'd say, like love and abandonment were the same thing.

Maybe they were. I wouldn't understand that until much later.

1982-1989 - Various Houses, Louisiana

The Johnsons kept me from eight months to two years old. Mrs. Johnson was kind in the way that exhausted people are kind—efficiently, without much extra energy for warmth. She had three other foster kids and worked double shifts at the chicken processing plant. I was fed, clothed, changed when necessary. I learned to sleep through crying and to cry quietly when I needed to.

The Martinezes came next. They spoke Spanish to each other and English to me, and I spent my toddler years caught between languages I barely understood. Mrs. Martinez taught me to fold washcloths and sort socks. Useful skills, she said. I'd need useful skills.

She was right about that.

By the time I was five, I'd lived in eight different homes. I kept count in my head first, then later in a little notebook I hid wherever I was staying. Each move got its own entry: *Martinez house - 14 months. They got pregnant. White family - 6 months. I wet the bed too much. Jackson house - 3 months. Mrs. Jackson said I was "difficult."*

I learned to read the signs early. The hushed phone calls with social workers. The way foster parents stopped making eye contact. The sudden appearance of my clothes, washed and folded, sitting on my bed like a quiet eviction notice.

1989-1991 - The Johnsons (Again)

When I was eight, they sent me back to the Johnsons. Mrs. Johnson was older now, grayer, with fewer foster kids and more patience. Or maybe I was just easier to handle—I'd learned to make myself useful, to anticipate needs before they were voiced.

"You're a good helper, Eliza," she'd say, and I'd feel proud of that. Being helpful was better than being difficult. Being useful meant you might get to stay.

I learned to change diapers and make bottles for the babies who came and went. I could fold fitted sheets and scrub bathtubs and make scrambled eggs that didn't stick to the pan. By the time I was ten, I was running the household better than some adults I'd known.

But even good helpers weren't permanent.

1991-1994 - The Washingtons

At eleven, I hit the jackpot: the Washingtons. Margaret and James Washington had been fostering kids for fifteen years, and they understood something the others hadn't—that broken things needed more than just basic maintenance to heal.

Mrs. Washington taught me to cook, really cook. Not just heat up frozen dinners or pour cereal into bowls, but to understand how ingredients worked together, how patience and attention could transform simple things into something nourishing. She let me help with the Sunday dinners she prepared for whatever kids were staying with them, and for the first time in my life, I felt like I was contributing to something bigger than just survival.

Mr. Washington helped me with homework and taught me to drive in their ancient Buick. He had gentle hands and a patient voice, and he never made me feel stupid for not knowing things other kids took for granted.

"You're smart, Eliza," he'd tell me when I struggled with math homework. "You just learn different because you've had to learn different things."

For two years, I let myself believe maybe this was it. Maybe I'd finally found the place where I belonged. The Washingtons talked about adoption, about making it official, about college scholarships, and future plans. I started calling them Grandma and Grandpa Washington. I started thinking of their house as home.

Then Mr. Washington had a stroke.

1994 - The End of Maybe

I was thirteen when it happened. One day, Mr. Washington was teaching me to parallel park, and the next he was in the hospital with tubes down his throat and machines doing what his body couldn't anymore.

Mrs. Washington spent every day at the hospital, holding his hand and talking to doctors and learning about physical therapy and speech pathology. She'd come home exhausted and empty, with nothing left to give a thirteen-year-old girl who needed more than just a place to sleep.

The social worker explained it to me gently. It wasn't personal. It wasn't my fault. It was just circumstances.

But at thirteen, getting moved again felt like the final confirmation of what I'd always suspected: I was the kind of person who got left behind. Even the good ones couldn't keep me.

1994-1999 - Aging Out

The last few foster homes blur together in my memory. The Garcias, who meant well but had four biological children and not much room for an awkward teenager. The Thompsons, who took in foster kids for the extra money and treated us accordingly. The Bennets, who were perfectly fine but perfectly temporary.

I learned to detach. To go through the motions of belonging without actually investing in the possibility of permanence. I did my chores, made decent grades, and counted down the days until I turned eighteen and could stop pretending that any of these places would ever be home.

I aged out of the system with a high school diploma, a small savings account from part-time jobs, and absolutely no idea what to do next. Most of my fellow foster alumni disappeared into minimum-wage jobs or early parenthood or the kind of survival that didn't leave much room for dreaming.

But I'd learned something in all those foster homes, something that would serve me better than I realized: I knew how to read people. I knew how to make myself useful. And I knew what it felt like to need someone to show up and stay.

1999-2003 - Becoming Useful

I used my savings and a Pell Grant to enroll in the nursing program at the local community college. It made sense—I'd spent my childhood taking care of people, learning to anticipate needs and solve problems quietly. Why not get paid for skills I'd been developing since I was eight years old?

The program was hard. Not just the science and the procedures, but the emotional weight of it. Watching people suffer, watching families fall apart, learning that sometimes the kindest thing you could do was help someone die with dignity instead of trying to save them.

But I was good at it. Really good. I understood something my classmates struggled with—that healing wasn't always about fixing. Sometimes it was just about showing up. About making sure no one had to face their worst moments alone.

2003-2018 - Finding Purpose

I worked hospital floors for fifteen years. ICU, emergency room, oncology—the hardest cases, the ones that made other nurses burn out after six months. But I thrived in those spaces where life and death brushed up against each other every day.

I became known as the nurse who could handle the difficult patients. The ones who were angry or scared or completely alone. The ones who reminded me, in some way, of myself.

Mrs. Patterson, ninety-three years old, whose children lived across the country and visited twice a year. I sat with her during her final weeks, listening to stories about the victory garden she'd planted during World War II and the husband she'd lost to Korea.

Marcus, twenty-six years old, dying of AIDS-related complications while his family pretended he didn't exist. I held his hand during his final hours and made sure his partner could say goodbye.

Sarah, sixteen years old, in a car accident that killed her boyfriend and left her paralyzed. I taught her how to transfer from bed to wheelchair and listened to her rage against a world that had changed forever in the space of a heartbeat.

Each patient taught me something new about resilience, about the different ways people learn to carry unbearable weight. But they also taught me something about myself: I was good at being needed. I was good at showing up for people who had been left behind.

2018 - The Call

"We have a special case," my supervisor said when she offered me the position with Magnolia Parish Hospice. "The family is... particular. The patient is strong-willed and probably won't like having a stranger in her house. But you're good with the difficult ones."

What she didn't tell me was that Opal Mae Rhodes wasn't difficult—she was just particular about who she let matter to her. And once you mattered to Opal Mae, you mattered forever.

October 2024 - Eight Months Until Present Day

I walked into that house on Magnolia Street expecting another professional relationship. Another patient who needed medical care and emotional support through the hardest chapter of their life.

Instead, I found Opal Mae sitting in her armchair, wearing a hot pink housecoat and a wig she'd named Doris, looking at me like I was there to steal her silverware.

"Well," she said, "you're not what I expected."

"What did you expect?" I asked, setting down my nursing bag.

"Someone older. More serious. Maybe with a mustache." She paused, considering. "Are you any good at this, or are you just here to watch me die?"

"I'm very good at this," I told her. "And I'm here to help you live as well as possible for as long as possible."

"Good answer." She pointed to the love seat across from her. "Sit down. Tell me about yourself. And don't give me any of that professional nonsense—I want to know who you really are."

So I told her. Not everything, not right away, but enough. About growing up in foster care and learning to make myself useful and finding my purpose in helping people through their hardest moments.

She listened without interrupting, those sharp eyes taking in everything I said and everything I didn't say.

"Well, Eliza Staunton," she said when I finished, "I think we're going to get along just fine."

October 2024 - June 2025

And we did. Better than fine. Over the next eight months, Opal Mae became the mother I'd never had, the family I'd spent my whole life searching for.

She taught me to make proper biscuits, though mine never turned out quite right. She showed me photo albums and told me stories about her daughters—their personalities, their quirks, their complicated relationships with each other and with her.

"Jo thinks she has to hold everything together," she'd say while I helped her with her medications. "But she's been holding so tight for so long, she's forgotten how to let go."

"Magnolia runs because she's afraid of being left behind. But she doesn't understand that sometimes you have to stay still long enough to let people catch up to you."

"Merritt thinks she doesn't belong, but she's the one who makes everyone else feel like they do."

"Wrenlee sees everyone's broken pieces and tries to put them back together. But who takes care of the caretaker?"

She worried about them constantly, these daughters she'd raised to be strong and independent and maybe a little too good at taking care of themselves.

But she also made me promise things. Important things.

"When I'm gone," she said one afternoon while I was brushing her hair—what was left of it after the chemo—"I want you to stay connected to my girls. They're going to need someone who understands what it means to choose your family instead of just being born into one."

"Mrs. Rhodes—"

"Opal Mae," she corrected, like she always did. "And I'm serious, Eliza. You belong with us now. Death doesn't change that."

June 18, 2025 - The End and the Beginning

She died on a Tuesday morning, holding my hand while the early summer light streamed through her bedroom window. Her last words were about her daughters—worry and love tangled together in her failing voice.

"Take care of my girls," she whispered. "They're going to think they're fine, but they're not. They need family. They need you."

I sat with her body for an hour after she was gone, holding her hand and crying for the woman who had given me something I'd never had before: unconditional love. Not because I was useful or helpful or good at anticipating needs, but simply because she had chosen to love me.

In the weeks that followed, I kept thinking about that last conversation. About her insistence that I belonged with her family, that death didn't change that. I'd helped families through grief before, but I'd always stepped back afterward, moved on to the next patient who needed me.

This time felt different. This time, I couldn't let go.

So when I heard through the hospice network that the daughters were gathering at the house to sort through Opal Mae's belongings, I knew I had to go. Not as a professional, but as someone who had loved her too. Someone who understood that family isn't always about blood—sometimes it's about choice.

I packed my terrible muffins and my unfinished scarf and drove to that house on Magnolia Street, hoping they'd understand what their mother had tried to tell me.

That I belonged there, too.

12

The Gift of Words

-Delilah-

Present Day - Saturday, 11:30am

The accordion incident had left everyone in surprisingly good spirits. Even Aunt Jo seemed more relaxed, her clipboard abandoned on the coffee table while she actually ate one of Eliza's terrible muffins without grimacing too much. It was nice to see everyone acting like, well, actual people instead of walking grief monuments.

I was back to my unnecessary dusting—a nervous habit I'd inherited from Mama, though I was pretty sure she'd gotten it from Gran—when Eliza suddenly stopped mid-stitch on her knitting project.

"OH!" she exclaimed, loud enough to make Aunt Merritt jump. "I completely forgot with all the fun chaos. I found a few of your mama's things, and I wanted to return them."

Aunt Magnolia groaned dramatically. "Uh uh! Don't you see how much stuff we still have to go through?"

But Eliza was already digging through her duffel bag with the determination of someone on a mission. "I definitely think you will want to at least look at this."

She pulled out what looked like a worn leather journal and held it reverently, like she was handling something precious. Which, judging by the way all the adults suddenly went very still, maybe she was.

"Is this Mama's journal?" Aunt Magnolia asked, her voice softer than it had been all morning.

"It is," Eliza confirmed. "I thought you'd appreciate some of the stories that she wrote."

Aunt Jo set down her muffin. "Well, read us one, Nolie."

Aunt Magnolia took the journal like she was receiving communion, flipping through pages with careful fingers. "Here's one about me! June 15th, 2005."

She cleared her throat and began to read, and I could hear Gran's voice in the words even though it was Aunt Magnolia speaking:

> *Magnolia called today from California. She said she met a man named 'Blade' who owns a goat farm and believes in reincarnation. Naturally, I poured a drink.*
>
> *She's always been the wild one, that girl. Left home with nothing but a suitcase full of scarves and more confidence than common sense. But I'll be damned*

if I don't admire her. She burns too bright to be tamed. Sometimes I worry that she'll run so fast she forgets where home is... but then she calls, and for a few minutes, I know she still belongs to me.

Also—who names a man 'Blade'? Is that a nickname? Is he in a gang? Or is he just sharp?

The laughter that followed was different from our earlier giggles—warmer, more bittersweet. Aunt Magnolia was holding back tears, and I could see why. Even when Gran was worried about her, even when she was clearly exasperated, the love came through in every word.

"She admired me?" Aunt Magnolia whispered. "Why didn't she ever tell me that? Ugh, that woman."

"Give it to me!" Mama said, reaching for the journal. "I want to find one."

She flipped through pages with the eager excitement of someone looking for treasure, and maybe that's exactly what this was—buried treasure in the form of their mother's private thoughts.

March 19th, 2021

It rained all day today. One of those soft rains that makes the world feel like it's trying to whisper something.

I made soup no one asked for. Sat in Melvin's chair. Listened to the wind get tangled in the windchimes I never had the heart to take down after he passed. I realized something while stirring that soup—grief is just love that doesn't know where to go. I still love him. I still make too much soup. I still wait for the door to open even though I know it won't.

But I also laughed today. Out loud. At one of my own jokes. I said, 'Opal Mae, you are one sassy widow,' and then I cracked up so hard I snorted into the split pea.

Progress.

Aunt Jo's hand went to her throat. "I don't know how many more of these I can take. Eliza, this is a real gift. Thank you so much for bringing this to us."

"Anytime, Jolene," Eliza replied, and there was something in her voice that suggested she meant it literally—anytime, anything, always.

"Oh hey, Merr," Mama said, still flipping through pages. "There is one in here about you, too. It's from your first birthday."

Aunt Merritt looked up from her coffee like someone had called her name in a crowded room. "Let me see that!"

She took the journal with hands that weren't quite steady and found the entry Mama had mentioned. When she started reading, her voice was soft but clear:

We threw Merritt her first birthday party today. The first one where she was ours. We went a little overboard, of course. Balloons, streamers, a purple dress she hated, and a cake so crooked it looked like it needed a prayer.

She didn't say much—quiet girl, always has been—but she looked up at me and smiled when we sang the birthday song. I mean, really smiled. Like she finally believed she belonged.

I worry sometimes that she feels like the outsider. That she thinks she was added to the story too late. But what she doesn't know—what I should've told her—is that she didn't join our family.

She completed it.

The silence that followed was the kind that feels sacred, like we were all holding our breath so we wouldn't disturb something beautiful and fragile. Aunt Merritt's eyes were bright with unshed tears, and I could see her fighting to keep her composure.

"I told you that you meant more to this family than you give yourself credit for," Mama said softly, moving closer to her sister.

Aunt Jo joined them, putting her arm around Aunt Merritt's shoulders. "She's right, Merr. You were like a missing piece to our family puzzle."

"That's right," Aunt Magnolia agreed, completing what was turning into a group hug.

Eliza, who had been watching this unfold with the kind of careful attention that suggested she understood exactly what she was witnessing, suddenly jumped up from her chair.

"Awwww! I love you guys!!!" she declared, throwing herself into the sister sandwich with such enthusiasm that everyone laughed even as they made room for her.

I stood there watching all these women—my mama, my aunts, and this new person who somehow fit right into our family chaos—and felt something shift inside my chest. It was like watching a broken thing put itself back together, not perfectly, but in a way that made it stronger than it had been before.

"Crazy how this little journal seems to have mended a broken piece inside of them," I said, more to myself than to anyone else, but loud enough that they could all hear.

And it was true. Gran's words, written in private moments when she thought no one would ever read them, had done what days of sorting through belongings and arguing over inheritance couldn't do. They'd reminded everyone that love doesn't disappear when someone dies—it just changes shape, becomes something you carry instead of something you receive.

The hug lasted longer than hugs usually do, like none of them wanted to be the first to let go. And watching them, I realized that maybe that was the real inheritance Gran had left us. Not the house or the belongings or even the memories, but this: the knowledge that family is something you choose every day, something you build with words and actions and the decision to keep showing up for each other, even when it's hard.

Especially when it's hard.

13

When The Time Comes

-Jolene-

Present Day - Saturday, 4:30pm

The afternoon had settled into a rhythm I was grateful for. We'd found our places in a circle on the living room floor, boxes scattered around us like archaeological sites waiting to be explored. Delilah had efficiently set up our sorting stations, and even Eliza had claimed a spot nearby with that eternal scarf of hers, sipping tea like she'd always been part of our family chaos.

I surveyed the progress we'd made and felt a small surge of satisfaction. "Alright, team. Deep breath. We've made it through half the hoard. Time to dig in again."

Magnolia groaned dramatically from her spot across from me. "If I find one more box labeled 'miscellaneous,' I swear I'm going to toss it without looking."

"That's how you miss the good stuff," Merritt warned, ever practical.

"Like the taxidermied squirrel in the pantry," Delilah added with a grin.

Wrenlee shuddered. "I'm still not over that."

Eliza looked up from her crocheting. "That squirrel had a name. She called it 'Sir Chippers.'"

"Of course she did," Magnolia muttered, but I could hear the fondness in her voice.

I reached for the next box, reading Mama's careful script on the label. "This one says, 'Important. Do Not Throw Away. Seriously.'"

"That could either be birth certificates or expired coupons," Merritt observed dryly.

"Only one way to find out." I opened the box and immediately felt my breath catch. Inside, nestled in tissue paper, was Mama's old jewelry box - the ornate wooden one with brass corners that had fascinated us as children.

"Oh wow... is that Mama's old jewelry box?" Wrenlee asked, leaning forward.

Magnolia's face lit up with recognition. "She used to let me play with that when I was sick."

"Me too!" Wrenlee exclaimed. "I thought it was real treasure."

"In a way, it was," Merritt said softly.

I lifted the box carefully, feeling its familiar weight. Inside, I found a note in Mama's handwriting. Despite everything we'd been through today, I couldn't help but smile as I read it aloud:

Dear girls: If you're reading this, I either died peacefully or dramatically. Either way, I'm still the main character.

We all laughed softly. Even in death, Mama managed to make us smile.

"God, I loved that woman," Eliza said with genuine affection.

I continued exploring the jewelry box's contents. "Here's her strand of pearls."

"The ones she wore to every church potluck," Magnolia remembered.

"And that one wedding where she got into a shouting match with the groom's mother," Wrenlee added.

Delilah looked curious. "What happened?"

I grinned at the memory. "Mama said, 'If your potato salad had seasoning, I'd keep my mouth shut.'"

"A true Southern icon," Merritt declared.

"She had zero fear of confrontation," Eliza observed.

"I think I got that from her," Magnolia said.

"We all got a little something." I held up a cassette tape I'd found in the box. "What's this?"

Merritt leaned over to look. "Let me see... That's one of her old voice journals."

"You mean she recorded herself instead of writing sometimes?" Wrenlee asked.

"Yeah. When her hands hurt too much to write."

Delilah's eyes brightened. "Can we listen to it?"

"We'll need a tape player," I said, already knowing the answer.

Eliza was already standing. "I've got one in my car. Don't ask."

Magnolia shook her head with amusement. "Why am I not surprised?"

While Eliza went to retrieve the tape player, we continued exploring the box. Wrenlee pulled out an old apron and held it to her nose. "Here's an old apron. Oh, wow, it still smells like cornbread."

The scent hit me like a wave of memory. "That was her comfort smell."

"Mine was her rose lotion," Magnolia said wistfully.

"Mine was the fireplace," Merritt added.

"She always smelled like lavender when I visited," Delilah said quietly.

When Eliza returned with the tape player, she set it up with the efficiency of someone who'd done this before. "Alright, plug your ears if you're not ready to cry."

She put in the tape and pressed play. Mama's voice came through the speakers, crackly but unmistakably strong, and I felt my heart clench with missing her.

March 4th. It's raining today. Good grief, I love the rain. Feels like the world finally sits still long enough for me to think. I made soup. It's terrible. But I made it.

We all listened in complete silence as her voice continued.

I miss my girls. Even when they're here, I miss them. Isn't that strange? How you can love people so hard your heart stretches too big to hold it all? I hope they know that I see them. All of them. Jo, with her lists. Merritt, with her quiet fire. Magnolia, with her firecracker mouth and soft-as-butter heart. Wrenlee, the glue, even when she doesn't know it. And little Delilah, who somehow sees the whole world with eyes older than mine.

The silence that followed felt sacred.

"I can't believe she included me in this," Delilah whispered, tears in her eyes.

"She loved you something fierce," I assured her.

"She really saw us," Magnolia said wonderingly. "Even when we didn't see each other."

"Or ourselves," Merritt added.

"I miss her laugh. That wheezy snort," Wrenlee said.

"I've been dreaming about it. Every night," I admitted.

Eliza looked up from her crocheting. "Grief is a funny house guest. Shows up, eats your food, never leaves."

"And still somehow, you'd miss it if it disappeared," Magnolia said.

Merritt reached for another item from the box. "Here's another journal."

"Her handwriting got so shaky near the end," Wrenlee observed sadly.

I took the journal and flipped through the pages until I found a short entry. "Let me see that... Here's a short one."

> *Merritt called today. Just to say hi. I cried for an hour. She'll never know how much that meant to me.*

Merritt's eyes filled with tears. "I didn't even say anything important."

"But you called. That's what mattered," Delilah said gently.

"I think we all underestimated how much the little things meant to her," Magnolia said.

"That's because she made them feel big. That was her gift," Eliza observed.

Wrenlee had been exploring another box and looked up with surprise. "I found another box. It says, 'Mama's Thoughts: For My Girls.'"

"That sounds ominous," Magnolia said.

"Or very on-brand," I replied.

"What's in it?" Merritt asked.

"Letters. Dozens of little letters. Some sealed, some not."

"She wrote us all letters?" Delilah asked in amazement.

"I told you she loved loudly," Eliza said with a knowing smile.

"Jo, you read one," Magnolia suggested.

I selected one of the unsealed letters. "Okay... this one says, 'To my girls, on a day when you need me.'" I opened it and began to read aloud:

> *If today's a hard day, know that I've had them too. Days when the sun felt too heavy. Days when my body ached and my spirit sagged. But I got through them. And you will, too. Because you are made of my bones. My laughter. My mistakes. My fire.*

"I needed that," Merritt said softly.

"We all did," Wrenlee agreed.

"She always knew what to say," Magnolia observed.

"Even now, she's holding our hands," Delilah said.

I looked around at my sisters, at the letters scattered between us, at the evidence of Mama's love spread across the floor. The letter I'd been carrying, the one addressed to me "for when the time comes," felt like it was burning a hole in my pocket.

The time had come.

"Well, I guess since we're all sitting here looking at letters... It's about time I opened the one Mama left for me for 'when the time comes.' I haven't read it yet. I just wasn't ready. But... I think I am now. I want to do this. Together."

The others gathered closer, and the room fell completely still. My hands trembled slightly as I opened the envelope that had been waiting for this moment.

I began to read aloud, my voice steady despite the tears threatening to blur my vision:

> *My dearest Jo. If you're reading this, then I've gone to glory—or at least somewhere with less laundry.*
>
> *The girls will be gathered. I hope you're sitting together, not across the room in silence. Look around you. These are your people. This is your circle.*
>
> *I know you, Jo. You're probably clenching your jaw right now. Trying to stay composed. But baby, let it out. You've held it together for everyone for so long.*

I paused to breathe, feeling the truth of her words.

> *You were the one I leaned on when things broke. When your daddy got sick, when I couldn't find the words, you stepped up. You always do.*
>
> *But Jo, strength doesn't mean silence. It doesn't mean loneliness. It doesn't mean doing everything alone.*
>
> *You've been mad at Magnolia for a long time. I know it. You think she left you. But what you don't know is she stayed longer than she thought she could. She stayed until her light started to go out. I told her to go. Because I needed her to find her spark again.*

I looked at Magnolia, stricken. "She wasn't ever supposed to tell you that," Magnolia whispered.

I continued reading:

> *I hoped you'd forgive her one day. That you'd understand it wasn't you she was running from—it was her own pain.*

"I always knew that," Wrenlee said quietly.

> *Merritt. You think you're background noise. You're not. You're the harmony that keeps this family's melody from falling flat. You were my miracle. Our lucky charm.*

Merritt was choking up. "I thought she forgot about that."

Magnolia scooted closer to comfort her as I continued.

Wrenlee. My glue. My soft-hearted peacemaker. You carry everyone's broken pieces. But baby, don't forget your own. Let them hold you sometimes.

"I will, Mama," Wrenlee said quietly.

Delilah. My hope. My next chapter. I see so much of your mama in you. Her courage. Her kindness. Her sass. You're the living proof that love outlives us.

"I love you, Gran," Delilah whispered, wiping away a tear.

And to all of you—stop fighting. Stop holding grudges like they're heirlooms. Let the pain breathe, but don't let it take up residence.

You're sisters. That means something. That means everything.

A deep, powerful silence settled over us as the weight of Mama's words sank in. Then, as if from everywhere and nowhere, her voice seemed to fill the room one last time:

If I know you girls, you're crying. Good. You should. Because grief is proof of love. Of life. Of connection.

But don't get stuck here. Don't linger in the past so long that you forget how to dance in the present.

Love each other. Hold each other. Let go of the weight. I left you my memories. Now, make your own.

You were my greatest adventure.

The silence that followed felt like a benediction, like Mama's arms wrapped around all of us one last time.

14

Jolene and Bobby

-Jolene-

2010-Present Day

I never believed in love at first sight until I saw Bobby Calloway trying to fix my broken printer at the accounting firm where I worked. It was March 15th, 2010 - a Monday that started like any other until the ancient HP LaserJet decided to eat half my tax season documents and jam spectacularly.

"Ma'am, I think your printer might be having an existential crisis," he said, looking up at me from where he knelt beside the machine, his sleeve rolled up and a streak of toner across his cheek. "It's questioning its life choices."

I should have been irritated. I had seventeen client files to print before my 2 PM appointment, and tax season waited for no one. Instead, I found myself laughing - actually laughing - for the first time in months.

"Can you perform printer therapy?" I asked. "Because I think it needs professional help."

"That'll be extra," he said with a grin that made my stomach do something entirely unprofessional. "But for you, I might make an exception."

Bobby worked for the IT company our firm contracted, and I'd seen him around before - tall, steady, with kind eyes and hands that seemed capable of fixing anything. But I'd never really *seen* him until that moment when he looked up at me and smiled like I was the best part of his Monday.

It took him three trips to fix that printer. Later, I'd suspect he broke it twice more just to have an excuse to come back.

"You know," he said during his final visit, "I don't usually ask this, but would you maybe like to grab dinner sometime? I promise not to talk about printers."

I almost said no. I was thirty-four, set in my ways, and had long ago decided that romance was for other people - people who didn't spend their evenings organizing receipts and color-coding filing systems. But something about the way he waited for my answer, patient and hopeful without being pushy, made me take a chance.

"Okay," I said. "But I'm warning you - I'm pretty boring."

"I doubt that," he replied. "Besides, I like boring. Boring is underrated."

Our first date was at a little Italian place downtown. I spent an hour getting ready, changing clothes three times before settling on a simple blue dress that Magnolia had insisted I buy months earlier. "You need more color in your wardrobe, Jo," she'd said. "Navy doesn't count as color."

Bobby was waiting when I arrived, and he stood up when he saw me - actually stood up, like we were in some old movie. No one had ever done that for me before.

"You look beautiful," he said simply, and I believed him.

We talked for three hours. About everything and nothing. He told me about growing up on his grandfather's farm, about learning to fish before he could properly ride a bike. I told him about my sisters, about Mama's tendency to keep everything and Daddy's quiet strength. He listened like my stories mattered, asking questions that showed he was really paying attention.

"You're the responsible one," he observed. "The one who keeps everyone else organized."

"Someone has to be," I said, automatically defensive.

"I'm not criticizing," he said gently. "I'm admiring. It takes strength to be the one everyone else leans on."

I'd never thought of it that way before.

When he walked me to my car, he didn't try to kiss me. Instead, he asked if he could see me again.

"I'd like that," I said, and meant it more than I'd expected.

Our second date was mini golf. Our third was a bookstore, where we spent two hours wandering the aisles and arguing about mystery novels. He liked the ones with complicated plots and red herrings. I preferred straightforward stories where everything made sense in the end.

"You want life to be organized," he said, not unkindly. "Even fictional life."

"Is that so wrong?"

"Not wrong. Just... exhausting. Don't you ever want to let someone else figure things out for a while?"

The question haunted me for weeks.

We'd been dating for six months when Daddy got diagnosed with lung cancer. I remember sitting in the oncologist's office, taking notes on treatment options while Mama cried quietly beside me and Daddy stared at the wall with that stoic expression he wore when the world got too heavy.

Bobby didn't push when I started canceling dates. He just showed up at the hospital with coffee and sandwiches, sitting in the waiting room doing crossword puzzles while I filled out insurance forms and talked to doctors. He never made me feel guilty for choosing family first.

"You don't have to stay," I told him one evening after a particularly long day of chemo treatments.

"I know," he said. "I want to."

"This isn't what you signed up for."

He looked at me then with an expression I was still learning to recognize - patient, steady, unshakeable. "Jo, I didn't sign up for easy. I signed up for you."

That was the night I knew I loved him.

Daddy responded well to treatment initially. We had two good years where the cancer seemed manageable, where life felt almost normal. Bobby became part of our family rhythms, showing up for Sunday dinners and helping Daddy with projects around the house. He and Mama developed an easy friendship built on their shared appreciation for terrible puns and their mutual dedication to taking care of me.

"He's good for you," Mama told me one afternoon as we watched Bobby and Daddy install new gutters. "You're less... wound up when he's around."

She was right. Something about Bobby's presence made me feel like I could breathe a little deeper, worry a little less. He had a way of stepping in when I was drowning in responsibility, not taking over but sharing the load.

When he proposed in December 2012, it was nothing like the elaborate gestures I'd seen in movies. We were sitting on Mama and Daddy's front porch after Sunday dinner, watching the sunset and listening to Daddy and Bobby argue about the best way to winterize the garden.

"Jo," he said quietly, "I want to spend the rest of my life taking care of you the way you take care of everyone else."

He pulled a simple ring from his pocket - white gold with a small, perfect diamond that caught the last rays of sunlight.

"Will you marry me?"

I said yes before he finished asking.

We married the following October in Mama's backyard, with white folding chairs and mason jars full of wildflowers. Daddy walked me down the makeshift aisle, his steps a little slower than they used to be but his grip on my arm steady and sure. Magnolia cried through the entire ceremony. Merritt took about a thousand pictures. Wrenlee made sure everyone had enough to eat. Delilah, then six years old, scattered rose petals with the serious concentration of someone performing brain surgery.

"You may kiss your bride," the preacher said, and when Bobby lifted my veil, his eyes were bright with tears.

"Hello, Mrs. Calloway," he whispered.

"Hello, husband," I whispered back.

The next seven years were the happiest of my life, even with the shadow of Daddy's illness growing longer. Bobby and I settled into a rhythm of quiet contentment. I kept my maiden name at work but loved being Mrs. Calloway everywhere else.

Bobby taught me things I didn't know I needed to learn. How to fish, though I was terrible at it and usually ended up reading while he cast his line. How to let him cook dinner without hovering in the kitchen, offering suggestions. How to watch a movie without folding laundry at the same time.

Most importantly, he taught me how to let someone else be strong.

When Daddy's cancer came back in 2018, more aggressive this time, I fell back into my old patterns - making lists, organizing medications, researching treatment options until 2 AM. But Bobby was there beside me, not trying to take over but making sure I ate, making sure I slept, making sure I didn't disappear entirely into the role of caregiver.

"You can't save him by sacrificing yourself," he said one night when he found me crying over my laptop, surrounded by printouts of experimental treatments.

"I have to try," I said. "I have to do something."

"You are doing something. You're loving him. That's enough."

But it didn't feel like enough when Daddy died on a cold Tuesday morning in 2020, the world already strange and scary with a pandemic none of us understood yet. We couldn't have the funeral we wanted, couldn't gather the way our family needed to grieve. Everything felt small and isolated and wrong.

I threw myself into settling Daddy's affairs, organizing his papers, helping Mama navigate the logistics of widowhood. Bobby let me, understanding that I needed to feel useful, needed to feel like I was honoring Daddy's memory by getting everything exactly right.

But at night, when the lists were made and the phone calls were finished, he held me while I cried. He didn't try to fix my grief or hurry me through it. He just held steady while I fell apart.

"I don't know how to do this," I confessed one night. "I don't know how to help Mama through this when I can barely handle it myself."

"You don't have to have all the answers," he said. "You just have to show up."

Mama struggled after Daddy died. She'd spent forty-seven years being half of something, and suddenly she was whole but alone. Bobby and I started spending more time at the house, sometimes staying overnight when she had particularly bad days. He never complained, never made me feel like I was choosing my family over our marriage.

Instead, he found ways to help that didn't feel like helping. He fixed the loose board on the front porch that had been wobbling for months. He taught Mama how to use the new smart TV so she could video call Delilah. He listened to the same stories about Daddy over and over, responding each time like he was hearing them for the first time.

"You know you married all of us, right?" I told him one evening after he'd spent three hours helping Mama reorganize her kitchen cabinets.

"Best deal I ever made," he said, and I knew he meant it.

The last five years with Mama were bittersweet. Good days when she was sharp and funny and fully herself, making us laugh with stories we'd heard a hundred times but still loved. Bad days when she forgot things, when she got confused, when she looked at us like she wasn't quite sure who we were. It didn't help that we had moved all the way to Knoxville for Bobby's job, and I sometimes had to leave him there on his own.

Bobby navigated it all with the same steady patience he brought to everything else. He learned which stories made her smile, which songs calmed her when she got agitated. He never talked down to her or treated her like she was fragile. He just adjusted his approach, the way he'd learned to adjust everything else in his life to accommodate the people he loved.

When Mama started getting really sick this past year, when it became clear that we were losing her by degrees, Bobby was the one who suggested I finally ask for help and allow hospice to come in for around-the-clock care.

"But it has to be me." I protested. "No one can take care of her like I will."

"Trust me," he said. "You can be particular about who helps you, but you *need* to let someone help."

He was right, of course. He usually was about the things that mattered.

Those last months were hard. Mama had good days and bad days, but she always knew us when we called or visited, though we never visited as frequently as we should have. She would tell us about her wonderful hospice nurse, Eliza, though we never seemed to cross paths. She would say that Eliza didn't want to interfere with *our* time. I never did get to truly thank her for loving Mama when we weren't able to be with her.

After Mama passed, when the funeral had come and gone, when the house felt impossibly empty and quiet, Bobby held me on the front porch swing while I cried fifteen years' worth of tears.

"I don't know who I am if I'm not taking care of someone," I whispered against his shoulder.

"You're Jo," he said simply. "You're my wife. You're Magnolia and Merritt and Wrenlee's sister. You're Delilah's aunt. You're a daughter who loved her parents well. That's enough. You're enough."

Now, sitting in this living room full of Mama's things, listening to her voice on that old recording, I understood something I'd been too busy to notice before. Bobby hadn't just taught me how to let someone else be strong. He'd taught me that love wasn't about being needed - it was about being wanted. Not because I could fix everything or organize everyone's life, but simply because I was me.

The irony wasn't lost on me that it had taken Mama's death to fully appreciate the gift she'd given me when she brought Bobby into my life. Or maybe the gift I'd given myself when I finally learned to accept his love without feeling like I had to earn it.

"You were my greatest adventure," Mama's voice said from the recording, and I understood now that she'd had many adventures. Marrying Daddy. Raising us girls. Watching us grow up and make our own families.

Bobby was mine.

And for the first time since we'd started this impossible task of sorting through a lifetime of memories, I felt ready to go home to him. Ready to let him hold me while I grieved. Ready to let him be strong so I could finally, finally let myself be soft.

15

More Boxes

-Wrenlee-

Present Day - Sunday, 7:00am

I'd been sitting in this kitchen chair since before dawn, wrapped in one of Mama's old robes, watching the sun creep slowly across the linoleum floor. Sleep had been impossible after yesterday - after hearing Mama's voice on that recording, after Jo read that letter aloud. My heart felt too full and too empty at the same time, if that made any sense.

The house felt different in the early morning quiet. Not just empty, but expectant, like it was holding its breath waiting for something to happen. I'd always been an early riser, but this morning I'd woken with a restlessness I couldn't shake, so I'd come downstairs to think.

That's when I heard Eliza's voice from outside, something about squirrels and traps, and despite everything, I had to smile. That woman was a force of nature, showing up exactly when we needed her most.

"Eliza! Good Lord! You scared me half to death," I said as she burst through the front door like a whirlwind in scrubs.

"Sorry, hun. I keep forgetting I move like a ninja before 8 a.m. You look like you haven't slept."

She wasn't wrong. "I didn't. Just sat here thinking."

"Well, I brought backup." She held up a brown paper bag like it contained the secrets of the universe. "Muffins, something that vaguely resembles coffee, and a deeply questionable yogurt that was half-off cause the label's in Spanish and I don't know what fruit it is."

"I'll take the mystery fruit," I said, grateful for the distraction.

Eliza immediately set to work, opening drawers and hunting for plates like she'd been living here for years. She moved with the easy confidence of someone who understood that sometimes people needed taking care of, whether they asked for it or not.

"It's too quiet in here," she observed as she started the coffee pot. "Your mama would've had music on. Or the news at full blast, talkin' back to the anchors like they owed her money."

That made me smile despite the ache in my chest. "She always liked the noise. She said silence made her nervous."

"It's too still in this house without her," Eliza said, her voice unusually serious. "Like the walls are holding their breath."

The coffee pot sputtered to life just as Jo appeared in the doorway, already dressed and carrying a notepad. Even in grief, my sister couldn't help but organize.

"Morning," Jo said, looking like she'd slept about as well as I had.

"Hey, Jo."

"Look who's up and already overachieving," Eliza observed.

"I'm not overachieving. I just couldn't sleep."

"You know they say the early bird gets the worm, but the exhausted sister gets a stomach ulcer."

Before Jo could respond, Magnolia stumbled into the kitchen like a beautiful disaster - hair sticking up at impossible angles, wearing pajama pants and what looked like a vintage concert t-shirt.

"Did somebody say pie?" she mumbled, rubbing her eyes.

"Morning, sunshine. No pie, but there's coffee," Eliza said, already pouring a cup.

"Yes, please." Magnolia slumped into the chair next to me, and I automatically reached over to smooth down her hair. Some habits never die.

"Merritt out walking again?" Jo asked, settling at the table with her notepad.

"Left before sunrise. Said she needed air." I'd heard her slip out while it was still dark, her footsteps careful on the creaky porch boards.

A few minutes later, Delilah appeared in the doorway, dressed but barefoot, pausing like she wasn't sure if she was interrupting something important.

"Hey, everybody."

"Hi, sweetheart. Are you hungry?" I asked automatically, the mother in me never fully at rest.

"Ooo, is there cinnamon toast?"

"No, but I have muffins!" Eliza announced.

"Yes, please. I am still trying to wake up. Who even gets up this early in the morning?"

"I do," I said.

"Me too," Eliza chimed in.

"Not me," Magnolia groaned. "But I heard people in the kitchen and have a serious FOMO."

"FOMO? What's that?" I asked.

"Fear of Missing Out," Jo supplied, looking pleased with herself.

"I'm surprised you know that," Magnolia said.

"Hey, I know things."

"Well, I didn't. Thanks for the vocab of the day," I said, filing the term away. Having a teenage daughter meant constantly learning new language.

"Eliza, these muffins are much better than the first ones you brought us," Delilah observed after taking a bite.

"They are store-bought," Eliza admitted.

"That's why."

"Hey, now."

"I'm just kidding, bestie. Well, kinda," Delilah grinned, and I marveled at how easily my daughter had adopted this quirky woman into our family circle.

"Okay, y'all. We have to get back to work if we are going to finish all these boxes," Jo announced, standing up with her notepad.

The thought of facing another day of sorting through Mama's life felt overwhelming, but I followed Jo and the others into the living room as Merritt came through the front door, looking windblown and peaceful.

"Well, good morning, sister! You were up and out early," Magnolia said.

"I just needed to take a walk and get some fresh air."

"Was it a nice walk?" Jo asked.

"It was. Talked to Mama."

"Oh? What'd she say?" Magnolia's voice was carefully casual.

"She told me to tell you the B word is a bad word."

"It may be bad, but it was one of her favorites," Eliza observed.

"What're we doing?" Merritt asked, settling into our familiar circle.

"Getting back to these boxes. They aren't going to sort themselves," Jo said, ever practical.

I looked at the box I'd claimed yesterday, already half-full of things I couldn't bear to part with. "This one is mine. Don't touch it."

"Wow, Mom," Delilah said with amusement.

"You hush."

Eliza stood up, stretching. "While y'all are going through these boxes, do you mind if I just roam around for a bit? I know Opal Mae wasn't my Mama, but she sure did feel like it all those months we were together."

"Of course! Let us know if you find anything you might like to keep," Jo said immediately.

"Really?"

"Sure! You took care of her when we couldn't be here. I'm sure she would've wanted you to have something to remember her by," I added, meaning every word.

"Y'all are awesome. Thank you!"

After Eliza left to explore, Jo picked up a box and set it on the coffee table. "Okay. Let's get back to work. First up, oh, this is one of my high school yearbooks."

"Oh wow, let me see that! Let's see what people said about you," Magnolia said, immediately grabbing for it. She read aloud in a sing-song voice: "JoJo, it was fun having you in Home Ec this year. I hope you have a wonderful summer. Signed, Louise."

"Well, that's nice," Merritt observed.

"Yeah, boring. Trash," Magnolia declared.

"I'll keep that, thank you very much," Jo said, clutching the yearbook protectively. "Next up... Oh, my gosh." She pulled out what looked like a hat shaped like a turkey.

"Is that... a hat?" I asked, squinting at the bizarre object.

"If it is, it was beaten with an ugly stick," Magnolia said.

Merritt opened her mouth, then closed it, then opened it again. "Wait. Wait. That's the Thanksgiving hat, isn't it?"

"Ding ding ding! Ladies and gentlefolk: The Turkey Crown," Jo announced triumphantly.

The memory hit me like a wave. "Mama made us wear that thing every year for pictures."

"I have repressed this memory," Magnolia groaned.

"I have photos. Hold, please," Merritt said, already pulling out her phone.

We all leaned in as she scrolled through old pictures, and Jo started snickering. "Magnolia had braces and a full-on unibrow."

"I was thirteen!"

"Didn't we use to draw names to see who had to wear it each year?" I remembered.

"Y'all remember the year Uncle Clay tried to deep fry it?" Jo asked.

"Yes! He said, 'If it's a turkey crown, we're gonna serve it crispy,'" Merritt recalled.

"He set off the smoke alarm and ruined the green bean casserole," Magnolia added.

"We kept the casserole and tossed the hat in the dryer. Mama was mad for a month," Jo finished.

We all laughed, the sound echoing in the room like it hadn't in days.

"Okay, this one's a keeper," I declared.

"I mean... It's ugly. But it's legendary," Merritt said.

"We frame it with the photo. Art installation," Magnolia suggested.

"Alright. Turkey Hat: Keep," Jo sighed, placing it gently on our growing pile.

Then her expression changed as she reached into the box again, pulling out something soft and faded. A light blue apron with tiny embroidered flowers and a faint grease stain near the pocket. "Opal" was stitched in careful cursive across the chest.

"Her Sunday apron," Jo said softly.

The mood in the room shifted immediately. This wasn't funny or nostalgic - this was Mama, real and present and gone.

"She wore that every Sunday. Biscuits and gravy mornings," I said, my voice barely above a whisper.

"She always tucked a dish towel in the pocket, even if she didn't use it," Magnolia added.

"I remember hugging her while she wore it. It always smelled like flour and Ivory soap," Merritt said.

"That's the pocket she used to sneak me caramels in when Daddy was on his 'no sugar in the house' kick," Jo said.

"She gave me her biscuit recipe once, and I still mess it up," Magnolia said.

"That's because she didn't write the important parts down. She just said things like 'til it feels right' and 'just enough to make the dough pray for mercy,'" I said, and we all chuckled gently.

"I found a letter in my Bible the other night. She wrote it to me in college. Said she hoped I'd find a kitchen I loved and a table full of people I wanted to cook for," Merritt said quietly.

Jo folded the apron carefully and laid it in her lap. "We can't toss this. I won't let us."

"Definitely keep," Magnolia agreed.

"We'll take turns holding onto it. Maybe one of us will finally crack the biscuit code," I suggested.

"Wouldn't that be something?" Jo said with a sad smile.

"Keep," Merritt said quietly.

Jo placed the apron beside the turkey hat, then reached back into the box and pulled out a small metal tin that jingled when she moved it.

"What on earth..."

"Is that... buttons?" Magnolia asked.

"No. Wait—it's those old state quarters. Remember when she tried to collect all fifty?" Jo said, opening the tin.

"She was obsessed. She used to harass gas station clerks," Merritt remembered.

"She once made me trade a perfectly good dollar for a quarter with Oregon on it," I said.

"And she never got Alaska," Magnolia noted.

Jo tilted the tin, confirming what we all knew. "Still no Alaska. Just like her dreams of visiting. She always said she wanted to see the Northern Lights."

"She never even flew on a plane," I said sadly.

"She always said, 'Y'all go further than I did. That'll be enough,'" Merritt quoted softly.

After a pause, Magnolia spoke up. "We should finish the collection."

"Send her to Alaska in spirit," I agreed.

"Put the complete set in the shadowbox we make for the apron," Jo said.

"Okay. So—keep the quarters?" Merritt asked.

"Keep," we all said in unison.

"Okay. The rest of this box seems to be a bunch of trashy romance novels," Jo announced.

"Donate!" we all shouted immediately.

"That was an easy one. Delilah, will you hand me another box?" Jo asked.

"Sure, Aunt Jo!" Delilah said, passing over a smaller box.

"Thanks, sweetie. Let's see what is in here. Oh, it's just a manila envelope. I wonder why they would've put this in a box on its own."

"Well, what is in it?" Magnolia asked.

Jo read the front of the envelope, and my heart stopped. "It's addressed to Wrenlee."

"To me?"

"Yep. 'To My Sweet Wren. You'll know what to do,'" Jo read, handing me the envelope.

My hands shook as I opened it. Inside was a deed - the deed to the house. And a note in Mama's handwriting that made my world tilt sideways.

"Good grief, Mama," I whispered.

"What is it, Wren?" Merritt asked, concern in her voice.

"Yeah, is everything okay?" Magnolia added.

I looked around at my sisters, at my daughter, at this room full of memories and love and complicated family history. The weight of what Mama had left me - the responsibility, the trust, the impossible decision - felt heavier than I could bear.

"Can y'all excuse me for a little while. I... I just need to be alone for a minute."

"You take as long as you need, honey. We will keep going through these boxes and put anything we think you'll want to keep in your box," Jo said gently.

"Thank you, Jo. I just— I need some air."

I headed for the front door, clutching the envelope like a lifeline, feeling my family's eyes on me as I walked away from everything I thought I understood about Mama's final wishes.

"I love you, Mama," Delilah called after me.

"And I love you, baby," I managed to say before stepping out into the morning air, where I could finally breathe again.

16

The Peacekeeper

-Wrenlee-

Present Day - Sunday, 8:00am

I settled onto the front porch swing with the envelope clutched in my hands, letting the morning air fill my lungs for what felt like the first time in days. The weight of Mama's final gift - or burden, I wasn't sure which - pressed against my chest like a stone.

The house deed. Made out to me. With that note in Mama's careful script: "To My Sweet Wren. You'll know what to do."

But I didn't know what to do. I'd spent eighteen years learning to make decisions on my own, learning to be strong when I didn't feel strong, learning to be both mother and father to my beautiful girl. And now this - this impossible choice that would affect not just me and Delilah, but all my sisters too.

I closed my eyes and let myself remember how it all started. How I'd ended up being the single mother, the one who had to leave Mississippi behind and start over in a place where nobody knew my story.

It was 2004 when I met Marcus Sinclair. I was twenty-three, fresh out of college and teaching kindergarten at Adalee Elementary, living in a little apartment fifteen minutes from Mama and Daddy's house. Life was simple then - work, family dinners on Sundays, the occasional Friday night out with other teachers. I thought I had everything figured out.

Marcus was new to town, working construction on the new shopping center they were building out on Highway 49. Tall, charming, with hands that could fix anything and a smile that made me forget my own name. He came into the diner where I sometimes ate lunch, always ordering the same thing - meatloaf and mashed potatoes, sweet tea, and a slice of coconut cake.

I was there grading papers one Tuesday afternoon when he finally worked up the courage to talk to me.

"You're a teacher," he said, sliding into the booth across from me without invitation. "I can tell by the way you hold your red pen like it might save the world."

I should have been annoyed by his presumption, but something about his easy confidence drew me in. Even then, I was already the peacekeeper - I'd rather accommodate than confront. "Kindergarten," I said. "And you're construction. I can tell by the way you smell like sawdust and possibility."

He laughed - a rich, warm sound that made other diners turn to look. "Possibility, huh? I like that. Most people just say I smell like work."

We talked for two hours that day. About his plans to start his own contracting business, about my dreams of maybe becoming a principal someday. He told me about growing up in Alabama, about his father walking out when he was ten, about learning to be the man of the house early. I told him about my sisters, about being the one who smoothed over their fights, about how I'd always been the one everyone came to when they needed problems solved.

"You're the peaceful one," he observed. "The one who keeps everyone else grounded."

"Someone has to be," I said automatically.

"What about what you want, though? Who takes care of you?"

The question caught me off guard. I'd never really thought about it that way.

Marcus pursued me with the same focused intensity he brought to everything else. Flowers delivered to my classroom. Little notes tucked under my windshield wipers. Sunday drives out to the lake, where we'd talk for hours about everything and nothing.

But it was how he handled meeting my family that really won me over. The first Sunday dinner at Mama and Daddy's could have been a disaster - Magnolia was in one of her dramatic phases, complaining loudly about her latest boyfriend's shortcomings. Jolene was stressed about some work deadline and snapping at everyone. Merritt was barely speaking, going through one of her quiet spells.

Marcus just... rolled with it. When Magnolia started ranting, he listened and asked thoughtful questions. When Jolene got sharp, he deflected with gentle humor. When Merritt stayed silent, he didn't try to force conversation but included her with smiles and small gestures.

"You're good at this," I told him later as we sat on the front porch. "Most people find my family overwhelming."

"They're not overwhelming," he said. "They're passionate. And they love you. I can see why you turned out to be such a peacemaker - someone had to learn how to speak all their different languages."

He fit seamlessly into our family chaos after that. Mama loved him because he complimented her cooking and actually listened to her stories. Daddy appreciated his work ethic and the respectful way he asked permission before taking me out. My sisters were charmed by his attention to detail - the way he remembered that Jolene liked her coffee black, that Magnolia was allergic to shellfish, that Merritt preferred listening to talking.

"He's good for you," Mama told me one Sunday after dinner while we watched him help Daddy fix a loose board on the back deck. "You smile more when he's around. You seem less worried about taking care of everyone else."

She was right. Something about Marcus made me feel lighter, more myself. Like I could stop managing everyone else's happiness long enough to focus on my own.

We were married in the fall of 2005, in a simple ceremony at the little Methodist church where I'd grown up attending Sunday services. I wore Mama's wedding dress. Marcus cried when I walked down the aisle, and Daddy had to steady him during the vows.

"You're my peace," Marcus whispered when the preacher pronounced us husband and wife. "My safe harbor."

For a year and a half, we were happy. We bought a little house two streets over from Mama and Daddy, with a big front porch and a garden where I grew tomatoes and herbs. Marcus's business was starting to take off - word spread about his quality work and fair prices. I loved teaching, loved coming home to a house that smelled like whatever Marcus was cooking for dinner.

We started trying for a baby right away. I'd always wanted children, and Marcus said he couldn't wait to be a father. When I got pregnant in early 2007, we were both over the moon.

"She's going to be beautiful," he'd say, his hand on my growing stomach. "She's going to have your eyes and your heart."

"What if it's a boy?" I'd tease.

"Doesn't matter. This baby is going to be perfect because it's ours."

Delilah was born on a cold February morning in 2007, after fourteen hours of labor that left me exhausted but elated. Marcus cried when the doctor placed her in his arms, this tiny, red-faced miracle with a shock of dark hair and lungs that announced her arrival to the entire maternity ward.

"Delilah Rose Sinclair," he whispered, and I fell in love with both of them all over again.

But something shifted after we brought her home. At first, I thought it was normal new-parent adjustment - we were both sleep-deprived, overwhelmed, learning how to be responsible for this tiny person who depended on us for everything. Marcus seemed nervous around Delilah, afraid he might hurt her, uncertain about how to hold her or calm her when she cried.

"You're a natural at this," he'd say, watching me change her diaper or rock her to sleep. "I don't know how you know what to do."

"I don't either," I'd laugh. "I'm making it up as I go along, just like you."

But as the weeks passed, instead of getting more comfortable, Marcus seemed to withdraw further. He started working longer hours, taking jobs farther from home. When he was with us, he seemed restless, distracted. The easy conversation that had always flowed between us became stilted, forced.

I told myself it was normal. That he was just adjusting to the responsibility of providing for a family. That he'd settle into fatherhood the way he'd settled into everything else.

I was wrong.

The night he left, Delilah was three months old. I was in the nursery, rocking her to sleep after a particularly fussy day, when I heard him moving around in our bedroom. By the time I got Delilah settled and went to see what he was doing, he had a suitcase on the bed, half-full of clothes.

"What are you doing?" I asked, though my heart already knew.

"I can't do this anymore," he said without stopping his packing. "I thought I could, but I can't."

"Can't do what? Be a husband? Be a father? What exactly is it you can't do, Marcus?"

He finally looked at me then, and I saw something in his eyes I'd never seen before - a kind of wild panic, like a trapped animal looking for escape.

"This isn't what I thought it would be," he said. "The crying, the diapers, the way everything revolves around her now. I can't breathe, Wren. I wake up every morning feeling like I'm suffocating."

"So we figure it out," I said, fighting to keep my voice steady. Even then, even as my world crumbled, my instinct was to smooth things over, to find a compromise. "We can get help. My family will pitch in more. We can hire a babysitter sometimes, have date nights—"

"No," he said, shaking his head. "You don't understand. This isn't about needing a break. This is about realizing I'm not cut out for this life. I thought I wanted it, but I was wrong."

"What about Delilah? What about your daughter?"

The question stopped him cold. For a moment, I thought I'd reached him, thought he'd remember who we were, what we'd built together.

"She's better off without me," he said finally. "Look at how good you are with her. You don't need me. You never really did."

"But I want you," I whispered. "She needs her father."

"I'm sorry," he said, and I could hear tears in his voice even though he wouldn't look at me. "I'm so sorry, Wren. But I have to go."

He left that night while Delilah slept in her crib, oblivious to the fact that her world had just changed forever. Left a note on the kitchen counter saying he'd gone to stay with a friend in Alabama, that he needed time to think.

I stood in our empty bedroom at three in the morning, listening to my daughter's peaceful breathing through the baby monitor, and felt something break inside me that I wasn't sure would ever heal properly.

The months that followed were a blur of survival. Mama and Daddy stepped in immediately, of course. Mama came over every day to help with Delilah while I tried to figure out how to be a single mother. Jolene created detailed schedules for feeding and sleeping and doctor's appointments. Magnolia brought over ridiculous outfits and toys, her dramatic nature temporarily channeled into fierce protectiveness of her niece. Merritt quietly took care of practical things - making sure I ate, helping with laundry, sitting with me during those long nights when I couldn't stop crying.

But as grateful as I was for their support, I also felt like a failure. The peacekeeper, the one who was supposed to have everything figured out - and I couldn't even keep my own marriage together.

"This isn't your fault," Mama told me over and over. "Some people just aren't built for the long haul."

"But I should have seen it," I said. "I should have known."

"How?" she asked. "He fooled all of us, honey. Even himself, probably."

The papers came six months later. Divorce papers filed from Alabama, with a note from Marcus saying he was signing away all parental rights. He didn't want custody, didn't want visitation, didn't want anything to do with the life we'd built together.

"At least now you know where you stand," Jolene said when I showed her the papers. "You don't have to worry about him showing up and trying to take her."

But I did worry. Because even though Marcus had legally walked away, I lived in constant fear that he might change his mind. That he might decide someday that he wanted to be part of Delilah's life, and I'd have to share my daughter with someone who'd already proven he couldn't be trusted with our hearts.

The final straw came when Delilah was eight months old. Marcus's mother called - a woman I'd met exactly twice during our marriage, who'd made it clear she thought her son was too good for a small-town Mississippi girl.

"I want to see my granddaughter," she announced without preamble.

"Your son gave up his parental rights," I reminded her.

"That doesn't change the fact that she's my blood. I have rights too."

The thought of this woman, who'd never shown any interest in Delilah before, suddenly deciding she had claims on my daughter made my stomach turn. But more than that, it made me realize something important: as long as we stayed in Mississippi, we'd never really be free of Marcus's shadow. At least not for a very long time.

"I think we need to leave," I told Mama one Sunday afternoon while Delilah napped in her playpen.

Mama looked up from the quilt she was mending. "Leave? What do you mean?"

"I mean, pack up and go somewhere far away. Somewhere Marcus and his family can't reach us. Somewhere Delilah and I can start fresh."

"Honey, you can't run from this."

"I'm not running," I said. "I'm choosing. I'm choosing to give my daughter a life where she doesn't have to wonder why her father didn't want her. Where she doesn't have to deal with grandparents she doesn’t know deciding they may or may not want a relationship with her."

The idea of leaving my family, leaving everything I'd ever known, should have terrified me. But it didn't. It felt like taking control of my story instead of letting other people write it for me.

My cousin in Sacramento - Daddy's brother's daughter - had been after me to visit for years. When I called and asked if she knew of any teaching jobs in her area, she didn't ask questions, just said she'd make some calls.

The offer came from an elementary school in a small town outside Sacramento three weeks later. The principal was a woman about my age and wanted to help.

"You don't have to do this alone," Jolene said the night before Delilah and I left for California. "We're your family. We're supposed to help each other."

"I know," I said. "And I love you all for wanting to help. But I need to prove to myself that I can do this. That I can be enough for her."

"You're already enough," Merritt said quietly. "You've always been enough."

But I needed to believe it myself.

The eighteen years that followed weren't easy, but they were ours. Delilah and I built a life in California - not the life I'd planned, but a good life nonetheless. I threw myself into teaching, eventually earning my master's degree and becoming one of the most requested kindergarten teachers in the district. Delilah grew up smart and funny and fiercely independent, never asking about her father because I'd learned to answer her questions honestly but simply: "Some people aren't ready to be parents, baby. But that doesn't mean there's anything wrong with you."

We came back to Mississippi for visits - Christmas, summer vacations, important milestones. But California was home now, the place where I'd learned to be strong in ways I'd never imagined I could be.

And now, sitting on this porch swing with Mama's final gift in my hands, I understood something I'd been too young and hurt to see before. Mama hadn't just left me this house because she trusted me to know what to do with it. She'd left it to me because she knew I was the one who understood what it meant to start over, to build something beautiful from the pieces of what was broken.

I thought about Delilah, inside with her aunts, about how she'd never known the fear I'd carried for so many years. How she'd grown up confident and secure, never doubting her worth because one person hadn't been strong enough to love her.

"You'll know what to do," Mama's note said.

Her confidence in me never wavered. I still don’t know what to do, or how I’ll tell my sisters, but I will figure it out. Just like I always do.

17

The Weight of Staying

-Jolene-

Present Day - Sunday, 10:00am

The silence in Mama's living room pressed against my chest like a hand pushing me underwater. I watched Wrenlee through the front window, her shoulders rigid as she stood on the porch, clutching that manila envelope like it held the secrets of the universe. Maybe it did. Lord knows Mama never was one to make anything simple.

"She's been out there a long time," Magnolia said, her voice cutting through the thick air.

"She needs space. Let's let her take it." The words came out steadier than I felt. Inside, every nerve was screaming. I'd been the one to handle everything—the funeral arrangements, the paperwork, the endless phone calls with lawyers and insurance companies. I'd been the executor, the responsible one, the daughter who stayed. And now Wrenlee gets handed some mysterious envelope that makes her look like she's seen a ghost?

Merritt's voice was barely a whisper. "She didn't even look at us when she left."

"She looked at the envelope." Magnolia's observation hit too close to home.

"And that's what matters, isn't it?" I couldn't keep the edge out of my voice anymore.

The house felt like it was holding its breath, waiting for something to break. I'd felt this way for days now—like I was walking on eggshells in my own childhood home, like one wrong word would bring the whole fragile structure of our family crashing down around us.

I found myself walking to the old thermostat, checking it out of habit, even though it hadn't worked in years. My hands needed something to do, something to control when everything else was spinning away from me.

"The air in this house always felt heavy," I said, running my fingers along the yellowed plastic.

"That was Mama's cooking," Magnolia offered, trying for lightness that neither of us felt.

"No. Even before that. It just… hung, like the house was holding its breath."

Magnolia's voice went soft. "Right now, I think it's grieving."

Something sharp twisted in my chest. "It's wood and nails, Magnolia." The words came out harsher than I intended, but I couldn't take them back. I couldn't afford to anthropomorphize this place, to give it feelings and intentions. If I started thinking of it as something alive, something that could hurt or be hurt, I'd never be able to make the hard decisions that needed making.

But Magnolia wasn't backing down. "So were her rocking chairs, but they would still sigh when you sat in them."

"That's because they were held together by wood glue and a prayer."

Merritt's voice was thoughtful. "She liked things that needed holding together."

"She liked people that way, too." The truth of it hit me like a punch to the stomach. Mama had always been drawn to the broken things, the lost causes, the projects that needed fixing. Including us. Especially us.

I moved to one of the boxes we'd been sorting through, transferring items from one container to another with mechanical precision. Each photograph, each knickknack, each worn piece of fabric—they all had stories attached, memories that would die with us if we didn't preserve them somehow. But preservation required space, required commitment, required staying.

"Y'all, we can't keep everything just because it has a story," I said, holding up a chipped ceramic angel that had sat on Mama's kitchen windowsill for as long as I could remember.

"Why not?" Magnolia's challenge was gentle but firm.

"Because we don't live here."

Merritt's voice was quiet but loaded. "Not yet."

The words hit the room like a stone thrown into still water, ripples of implication spreading out in all directions. My head snapped toward her, heart suddenly hammering.

"What does that mean?"

"I'm just saying we don't know what Wrenlee's holding."

Panic clawed at my throat. "What could possibly be in that envelope that would make us all of a sudden need to live here?"

But even as I said it, I knew. Deep in my bones, I knew. Mama wouldn't have made Wrenlee carry that envelope like the weight of the world unless it contained the weight of the world. For us, anyway.

Merritt was still talking, her words coming faster now. "I don't know. That's what I'm saying. We don't know what is in that envelope. It could be nothing. But, it could also be something. I mean, did you see the way she got up and walked out of here? It was like she'd seen a ghost."

"Oh, Merritt. Let's not waste time on ghost stories." But my voice sounded hollow even to my own ears.

Magnolia was studying me with those eyes that had always seen too much. "Jo, why do you feel the need to rush through all of this?"

The question stung because it was fair. Because underneath all my practical concerns about plumbing and roof repairs and property taxes, there was something else driving me forward. Fear. Fear that if we stayed in this emotional limbo too long, we'd never find our way out.

"I'm not rushing. I'm just handling it."

"You're controlling it."

Merritt's words were a slap of truth I wasn't ready for. "Someone has to."

The silence that followed felt absolute. Even the old house seemed to pause its creaking and settling, as if waiting to see what would break first—the floorboards or our family.

Magnolia's voice was barely above a whisper. "Does it feel different in here to y'all? Like Mama is watching us to see what we will do?"

I almost laughed. Almost. "I hope she is. Maybe she'll finally say something useful."

"Don't start, Jolene."

"What? Mama was many things. 'Direct' wasn't always one of them." The frustration that had been building since we arrived finally found its voice. Mama had been a master of the meaningful look, the loaded silence, the cryptic comment that left you guessing at her true intentions for years afterward.

"She had her reasons," Merritt said loyally.

"Which she took with her." The bitterness in my voice surprised even me.

Magnolia gestured to the boxes surrounding us like cardboard monuments to our mother's life. "She left more than you think."

Another pause. Another moment for doubt to creep in around the edges of my certainty.

"What if Wrenlee decides not to tell us what it is?" Merritt's question voiced what we were all thinking.

"Then she's being selfish." The words were out before I could stop them, sharp and cutting in the still air.

The front door opened, and Wrenlee stepped back inside, her face pale but composed.

"I'm not trying to be selfish, Jo. I promise."

Guilt crashed over me in a wave. "Oh, honey. I'm sorry. I know you aren't. I think all of this is just really starting to get to me."

And it was. All of it. The funeral, the endless decisions, the weight of being the one everyone looked to for answers when I felt just as lost as the rest of them. I'd been holding it together through sheer force of will, but the cracks were starting to show.

Magnolia's voice was gentle. "You okay, Wren?"

Wrenlee nodded, but I could see the exhaustion in the set of her shoulders. "This is just a lot."

“We need a dance party!!” Magnolia said with absolute excitement.

Despite the grief and the tension and the growing certainty that our world was about to shift on its axis, I found myself almost smiling. Almost.

"Magnolia, we are all too old for this."

But Merritt and Wrenlee were game, and soon Chubby Checker was blasting from Mama's old cassette player, and for just a moment, we weren't four grown women drowning in grief and responsibility. We were sisters again, daughters again, young enough to believe that dancing could fix anything that was broken.

The moment continued when Eliza and Delilah returned with coffee and tea, joining our impromptu celebration with raised eyebrows and amusement.

When Delilah went to turn off the music, reality came crashing back. The boxes. The house. The envelope still clutched in Wrenlee's hand like a ticking bomb.

"So what's the plan?" I heard myself saying. "We all just sit around until the tea and coffee tell us what to do? Or maybe we dance some more?"

"Jo, I'm not ready," Wrenlee said, and I heard the plea in her voice.

But I was done waiting. Done tiptoeing around whatever truth Mama had left for us to discover. "We need to have this conversation anyway."

"Here we go..." Magnolia's sigh was resigned.

I tried to soften my approach, tried to find the words that would make them understand without making me sound like the villain. "Look, I'm not trying to steamroll anybody. But this house—it's not just some relic. It's old. It's creaking."

"She hasn't been gone two weeks," Merritt protested.

"Exactly. Which means decisions need to be made before it turns into a museum of cobwebs and guilt."

"It is still her home," Magnolia said fiercely.

"No, Magnolia. It *was* her home."

The correction hung in the air like a challenge. Because that was the heart of it, wasn't it? The difference between was and is, between past and present, between holding on and letting go.

Eliza's dry observation about tattooing "Handle With Care" on our foreheads almost made me laugh despite everything. Again… Almost.

"Jolene, what is it you actually want?" Magnolia's question was direct, cutting through all the pretense.

I took a breath, tried to find the truth underneath all the practical concerns. "I want to stop walking around this house and hearing the floor moan every time someone shifts their weight. I want to stop worrying about mold and plumbing and what's going to collapse first."

I paused, felt the weight of their attention, their judgment, their need for me to be something other than what I was.

"And I want to stop feeling like the bad guy for saying any of that out loud."

Because that's what I'd become, wasn't it? The practical one. The responsible one. The one who had to think about property taxes and maintenance costs while everyone else indulged in sentiment and nostalgia.

"You're not the bad guy," Merritt said gently.

"We just... don't agree," Magnolia added.

Wrenlee's voice was quiet but loaded with years of family history. "That's the problem. We never did."

Never had truer words been spoken. We'd been four different people trying to love the same woman, trying to navigate the same family dynamics, trying to make sense of the same childhood that had somehow produced four completely different perspectives on what mattered and what didn't.

Eliza's comment about family being "a delightful stew of mismatched spices" was apt. Sometimes the flavors complemented each other. Sometimes they clashed so violently you couldn't taste anything else.

"Sometimes, it just boils over," Delilah added quietly.

"I don't want it to boil over. I just want it to go somewhere," I said, feeling the exhaustion in my bones. We'd been circling the same conversations, the same conflicts, the same unresolved tensions for days now. For years, really.

That's when Wrenlee dropped the bomb.

"Well, luckily, that isn't really your decision to make anymore."

The words hit like a physical blow. I felt all the air leave my lungs as everyone turned to stare at her.

"And what do you mean by that?"

But I already knew. Even before she said the words, I knew.

"I mean, the decision has been made for you. Mama left me the house." She held up the envelope like evidence in a trial. "She made the decision for all of us. This is the deed to the house, and apparently, I am supposed to know what to do with it."

The room tilted. Everything I'd thought I understood, every assumption I'd built my plans around, crumbled in an instant.

"She left it to you?" The words came out quiet, sharp, edged with all the hurt and confusion I was trying to keep buried.

"Yes. It's in writing. It's…official."

Official. Legal. Final. All the things I thought I'd been handling, all the responsibility I thought was mine by virtue of being the executor, the practical one, the daughter who'd stayed and sacrificed and handled things—none of it mattered.

Magnolia's voice cut through my spiraling thoughts. "Wait—wait just a damn second. Why you? Why not all of us?"

"I don't know. She didn't say. Just... 'To my Sweet Wren. You'll know what to do.'"

"You'll know what to do. Of course. Of course she said that to you. Her little glue stick."

The words came out bitter, loaded with years of watching Mama turn to Wrenlee for comfort, for understanding, for the kind of emotional connection that had always seemed just out of my reach. Wrenlee had been the peacemaker, the one who smoothed over conflicts and held the family together with her gentle presence and infinite patience.

I'd been the one who handled the paperwork.

The conversation devolved from there, all our carefully buried resentments and hurts spilling out like poison from a lanced wound. Merritt pointing out the cruel irony of me being executor but not inheriting. Me finally saying what we'd all been thinking—that I hadn't been enough. That despite everything I'd done, everything I'd sacrificed, it still hadn't been enough.

"I did everything. I stayed. I handled the paperwork. I cleaned out her fridge. I held her hand when Daddy died. I kept this family stitched together while Magnolia ran off to find herself, Wren was comforting Delilah, and Merritt..." I paused, looking at my youngest sister with eyes that suddenly saw too clearly. "Merritt was just always... there. On the sidelines."

But Merritt wasn't having it. Wouldn't let me diminish her experience to make sense of my own.

"I was never just there. I was trying so hard not to take up space. I didn't even know if I was allowed to want a piece of this place. You all had your baby blankets and dance recitals and shared memories—I had secondhand stories and casserole duty."

Magnolia was angry. Wrenlee was trying to remind us of Mama's tape recording, and that she 'saw' us. I was lashing out at Magnolia for all the times she'd left, all the times Mama had sat waiting for a daughter who never came home.

It was Delilah who finally stopped us. Sweet Delilah, who'd watched our family implode from the sidelines, who'd had to grow up too fast because the adults in her life couldn't figure out how to love each other without causing pain.

"Enough! Do you even hear yourselves? She's gone. She died. And you're all tearing each other apart like there's a prize at the bottom of the grief box."

As she stormed off, the silence that followed felt like the aftermath of an explosion. All the words that couldn't be taken back hanging in the air between us, all the damage that couldn't be undone spreading out like cracks in glass.

Wrenlee's voice was small, broken. "I didn't ask for this."

"You still got it." The words came out before I could stop them, before I could soften them with explanations or apologies.

Because that was the truth, wasn't it? She hadn't asked for it, but she'd gotten it anyway. The house, the responsibility, the final proof of Mama's trust and confidence. Everything I'd thought was mine by right of staying, of sacrificing, of being the responsible one.

"She gave me the deed, yes, but it's not a gift. It's a burden," Wrenlee said, and I believed her.

But Magnolia wasn't done. "Then why pretend to be the peacemaker? Why act like you're so above all of this when you're just as broken as the rest of us?"

My voice came out as a whisper, barely audible even to myself. "She really left it to you."

"She did."

Magnolia sat down hard, the fight going out of her like air from a punctured balloon. "Well... damn."

Well, damn indeed.

As the day moved on and left us sitting in the wreckage of our family's careful pretenses, I found myself thinking about weight. The weight of staying, of being responsible, of holding things together when everything wanted to fall apart.

I'd carried that weight for so long I'd forgotten how heavy it was. Had forgotten that maybe, just maybe, it wasn't mine to carry alone.

Maybe Mama had known that. Maybe she'd seen what I was too tired to see—that sometimes the person who handles everything isn't the person who should inherit everything. Sometimes they're just the person who needs to learn how to let go.

The thought should have been liberating. Instead, it felt like drowning.

Outside, the Sunday morning sun continued its climb toward noon, indifferent to our family drama, indifferent to the way our world had just shifted on its axis. Inside, four sisters sat surrounded by the boxes and memories of a woman who'd loved us all imperfectly but completely, trying to figure out how to move forward when the map we'd been following had suddenly been redrawn.

The weight of staying, I realized, was nothing compared to the weight of letting go.

But maybe—just maybe—it was time to learn the difference.

18

Watching Over

-Opal Mae-

Present Day - Sunday, 1:30pm

My sweet girls. I know they are hurting. Oh, how I wish that I could wrap them all up in my arms right now. But death, it turns out, can feel like a one-way conversation. I can see everything—feel everything—but I can't touch, can't speak, can't wrap them in the comfort they so desperately need.

So I watch. I listen. And I love them from a distance that feels both infinite and paper-thin. I hope they know I am still with them.

In the bedroom that used to be mine, Magnolia sits on the edge of the bed where I spent my final weeks. Her fingers trace the faded pattern of the quilt her grandmother made, and I can feel her searching for something—some piece of me she might have missed, some sign that she mattered more than she fears she did.

"Well, Mama…" Her voice cracks on the word, and my heart breaks all over again. "You always did like a good twist ending."

Oh, my wild, beautiful girl. If only you knew that every ending was just the beginning of something else. Every goodbye was really a "see you later." Every twist was just love finding a new way to reveal itself.

In the kitchen, Jolene stands at the sink, her hands gripping the counter so tightly her knuckles have gone white. She's staring out the window at the bird feeder I used to fill religiously every morning, watching the cardinals and blue jays fight over the last of the seeds. I know she's been meaning to refill it. I know she won't. It would feel too much like taking my place.

"I don't even know why I'm surprised," she says to the empty air, her voice steady but hollow. "You never made things easy."

No, sweetheart, I didn't. But easy was never the point. Growth, understanding, love that runs deep enough to weather any storm—those things require a little complexity.

Back in the bedroom, Magnolia's voice turns raw. "You left her the house. Wrenlee. Your 'sweet Wren.' And maybe she deserves it. Maybe she always did. But it still feels like a slap in the face."

I want to tell her it wasn't about deserving. It was about knowing. Knowing who would carry the weight without breaking, who would see the house not as a prize but as what it truly was—a place where love lived, imperfect and complicated and real.

Jolene's words drift from the kitchen, sharp with hurt. "You handed the keys to the only one who never asked for them. I wonder if you knew how that would sting."

Of course I knew, baby girl. Of course I knew it would hurt. But sometimes hurt is the only way to crack open a heart that's been closed too long, to let the light in where it's needed most.

"Was I too much? Or not enough?" Magnolia's question hangs in the air like smoke. "Did I burn too bright… or just burn out?"

Neither, my darling. You burned exactly as you were meant to burn. Fierce and wild and beautiful, lighting up every room you entered, even when you couldn't see your own glow.

The silence stretches, and I feel her gathering courage for the next words. "I know I ran. But I came back, Mama. Doesn't that count for something?"

Everything. It counts for everything. Every step you took away from home was a step toward finding yourself. Every mile you traveled was proof that my love could stretch across any distance. And every moment you chose to come back was a gift I treasured more than you'll ever know.

In the kitchen, Jolene's voice breaks through my thoughts. "I stayed. I stayed when everything felt like it was sinking—And still, you left the legacy to someone else. What more did I have to prove?"

Nothing, sweet girl. You never had anything to prove. Your staying wasn't a test—it was a choice, and it was beautiful, and it was enough. More than enough. But staying isn't the same as living, and living isn't the same as letting go. I needed to teach you that it was okay to stop carrying the world on your shoulders. That you could trust others to hold what mattered.

Magnolia's voice turns softer, more vulnerable. "You always told me I was the wild one. The mess. But I thought maybe—maybe—there was still room for me here. Not just in the house. In you."

Oh, my precious girl. You were never a mess. You were a masterpiece in progress, a work of art that couldn't be contained by conventional frames. And there was always room for you. In the house, in my heart, in every corner of the life we built together. The room was there—it was always there. You just couldn't see it through the smoke of your own burning.

From the kitchen comes Jolene's broken whisper: "You left me holding the threadbare rope, and now I'm not even sure I tied the right knots. Was I just the temporary glue while you decided who was worthy?"

The rope wasn't threadbare, honey. It was strong because you were holding it. And you weren't temporary anything. You were the steady heartbeat that kept us all alive when we might have otherwise fallen apart. But even the strongest hearts need to learn when to rest, when to let someone else take a turn carrying the weight.

"Did you think I wouldn't want it?" Magnolia asks, almost laughing through her tears. "That I wouldn't care?"

I knew you'd want it. I knew you'd care. I also knew that wanting and caring weren't the same as needing. You needed freedom, baby girl. You needed to know that love didn't require staying in one place, that belonging wasn't about possession but about understanding.

"Did you think I wouldn't be hurt?" Jolene's question cuts through the house like a blade.

I hoped you'd understand. Eventually. I hoped you'd see that being hurt was part of healing, that disappointment could crack open spaces for new kinds of joy. But hope and knowing aren't the same thing, and I know I asked too much of all of you.

"Maybe you thought Wren could keep us together better than the rest of us ever could," Magnolia says, and there's something like acceptance in her voice now.

"Maybe you were right," Jolene echoes from the kitchen.

Not better, my loves. Different. Wrenlee has the gift of seeing wholeness in broken things, of finding the center that holds when everything else is spinning apart. But each of you has gifts—Magnolia's fire that lights the way forward, Jolene's strength that holds the foundation steady,

Merritt's gentle wisdom that heals what seems beyond repair.

"I wanted to be part of the foundation," Magnolia says softly, "not just the firecracker who shook the windows."

You were both, sweetheart. You were the excitement that made life worth living and the passion that reminded us all what we were fighting for. The foundation needs firecrackers just as much as it needs steady stones.

Jolene's voice turns desperate. "You always saw me as the planner, Mama… But, did you ever really see me?"

I saw you, baby girl. I saw the little girl who organized her crayons by color and the teenager who made sure everyone got home safe and the woman who held our family together when everything wanted to fall apart. I saw your strength and your stubbornness and your incredible capacity for love, even when it cost you more than you could afford to give.

"Is this what you meant by teaching us a lesson?" Magnolia asks. "'Cause I'm learning, alright. I'm learning that coming home doesn't always mean belonging."

Home isn't a place, my wild one. It never was. Home is the love that follows you wherever you go, the acceptance that doesn't require you to be anything other than exactly who you are. You've always belonged—to me, to this family, to the wide world that needs your particular kind of light.

"I don't even know what to do now," Jolene admits. "Do I fight this? Let it go? Or just… pack a box and pretend it doesn't matter?"

Let it transform you, honey. Let it teach you that your worth isn't measured by what you inherit or what you control. Let it show you that love multiplies when it's shared, that legacy isn't about possession but about the imprint you leave on the hearts you touch.

"If you're listening… I need you to know I tried. I really did try," Magnolia whispers, and I want to shout back that I know, I know, I've been watching every brave step you've taken.

"Maybe you knew I was tired," Jolene says. "Maybe you knew I didn't have much left to give. Is that why you chose Wrenlee? I'm trying to understand. I am trying, Mama."

I see you trying, sweet girl. I see the exhaustion in your bones and the way you've been running on empty for too long. I chose Wrenlee because she could carry what needed carrying without it breaking her spirit. I chose her because she understood that the house was never really about the house at all.

The bedroom and kitchen fall quiet, my daughters lost in their own thoughts, their own grief. I desperately want to tell them that they're all enough, that they've always been enough, that my love for them isn't diminished by distance or death or the complicated mathematics of inheritance.

But then my attention shifts to the living room, where my youngest sits alone on the couch—the same couch where she used to curl up as a little girl, small and quiet and watchful.

"Hey, Mama," Merritt says to the empty room, and her voice is different from her sisters'—calmer, sadder, but somehow more at peace. "I know you probably have front-row seats to the emotional demolition derby happening in this house right now… and I'm just here… on the couch. Right where I always ended up. Not because I wasn't invited in… but because it's where I felt safest."

My heart swells with love for this daughter who always understood more than she let on, who found her place in the quiet spaces between everyone else's chaos.

"I guess some habits don't fade," she continues, and there's gentle humor in her voice.

She reaches for the envelope on the coffee table—the one that's caused so much pain today—and holds it gently, like it might contain something fragile.

"I know why you gave the house to Wren. I do. She's got your patience. Your heart. She's the one who could take something falling apart and somehow make it feel like it was always meant to be held that way."

Yes, my perceptive girl. Yes, you do know.

"So, no… I'm not mad."

Relief floods through me. At least one of my daughters understands. At least one of them sees the love beneath the decision.

"Jolene's hurting. Magnolia is too. They each wanted something—recognition, belonging, peace—and somehow that deed became all of it, rolled into one piece of paper."

She pulls the deed from the envelope, studies it with curious eyes rather than hungry ones.

"But me? I never needed the deed. I just needed the invitation. And you gave me that, Mama. When you let me draw all over that VHS tape… when you and Daddy called me your lucky charm, even when I was just a scared little girl trying not to break the family I'd been given."

Oh, Merritt. My lucky charm indeed. The daughter who taught me that sometimes the greatest gift you can give someone is simply letting them know they belong.

Her voice grows softer, more intimate. "I never told you this, but… there were nights—long after bedtime—I'd sneak into the living room and just sit on this couch because the house made a sound when everyone was sleeping."

I remember those nights. I remember sensing her small presence in the darkness and choosing not to check on her, knowing somehow that she needed those quiet moments, that solitude in a house full of noise.

"It wasn't creaks or wind or anything spooky. It was like… humming. Like the walls were singing lullabies to each other."

The house did hum, didn't it? With love and life and the gentle rhythm of a family breathing together in sleep. I'm so glad she heard it too.

"That's how I knew it was home. Not because I was born here. But because it loved me back."

Yes, baby girl. Yes, it did.

"So, no—I don't need a deed. I have something better. I have proof that I belonged. Right here. On this couch. Wrapped in your loud, messy, beautiful love."

A tear rolls down her cheek, but she doesn't wipe it away. She lets it fall like a blessing, like acceptance, like grace.

"That's all I ever wanted. That's all I ever needed."

She starts to put the deed back in the envelope, and that's when she sees it—the sticky note I placed on the back, the one I hoped would be discovered at just the right moment, when hearts were raw enough to receive what I had left for them.

"What's this?" she says, reading silently. I watch her eyes widen, watch understanding dawn across her face like sunrise.

"Oh my gosh. You guys!! Get out here!!!"

Her voice rings through the house, urgent and excited and full of the kind of hope that can change everything in an instant. I hear footsteps rushing from the kitchen and bedroom, hear my daughters' voices calling back to her.

And I smile because sometimes the smallest revelations contain the largest truths, and sometimes the most important conversations happen after we think we've said everything there is to say.

My girls are about to learn that love always has one more surprise up its sleeve, one more gift to give, one more way to prove that letting go and holding on aren't opposites after all.

They're just different sides of the same beautiful, complicated truth.

I watch and wait for them to discover what I knew all along—that the real inheritance was never about the house at all.

It was about each other.

19

The Gift Unwrapped

-Merritt-

Present Day - Sunday, 2:00pm

"What's this?" I said, staring at the small yellow sticky note on the back of the deed. The handwriting was unmistakably Mama's—that careful cursive she'd learned in Catholic school and never abandoned, even when arthritis made it shaky.

My heart started racing as I read the words. Then I read them again to make sure I wasn't seeing things.

For once in my life, I was the one with the answer. Me. Merritt. The one who usually sat quietly on the sidelines while my sisters fought and made up and fought again. But here I was, holding the missing piece of the puzzle that had been tearing our family apart for the past few hours.

"Oh my gosh. You guys!! Get out here!!!"

The sound of feet pounding across hardwood floors filled the house. Jolene appeared first, her face flushed with worry, followed by Magnolia, who looked like she'd been crying. Wrenlee and Delilah rushed in together, with Eliza bringing up the rear.

"What is it, Merritt? Are you okay?" Jolene's protective instincts kicked in immediately, scanning me for signs of injury or distress.

"I sure hope this is good," Magnolia said, pressing a hand to her chest. "You scared me half to death."

I looked around at my family—my beautiful, complicated, stubborn family—and felt a surge of something I hadn't experienced in years. Power. Not the cruel kind that comes from having something over someone, but the good kind. The kind that comes from being able to fix something that's broken.

"Y'all are going to want to sit down. Especially you, Wren."

"Just tell us what's wrong," Jolene demanded, still standing with her hands on her hips.

For once in my life, I wasn't going to be rushed. For once, I was going to make them wait for me. "Jolene, for once—just this time—do what you're told."

The look of surprise on her face was worth everything. "Well, yes, ma'am."

They all settled around me on the couch and chairs, leaning forward with anticipation. I savored the moment—all eyes on me, all attention focused on what I had to say. This was what it felt like to be essential, to hold something that mattered.

"Okay, we're seated. What is it?" Wrenlee asked, and I could hear the exhaustion in her voice. This whole weekend had taken a toll on all of us.

I took a deep breath, gathering my courage. "Mama didn't leave you the house!"

Magnolia's face crumpled with concern. "Oh, Lord. She's still in shock."

"No, I'm not! She didn't leave her the house!"

"And what makes you think that?" Jolene's voice had that edge it got when she thought someone was being ridiculous.

Wrenlee looked confused. "Yeah, Merr. I saw the deed."

"Did you look at the back of it?"

"Well, no…"

"Then you didn't see the sticky note?"

"What sticky note? What is going on??" Jolene was practically vibrating with impatience, but I wasn't going to be hurried. Not today.

"I'm getting to it! Patience, Jo. This is my moment. FINALLY."

And it was my moment. After years of being the quiet one, the one who watched their conflicts instead of creating them, I finally had something earth-shattering to share. I was going to milk every second of it.

"Come on, Merritt," Magnolia pleaded. "You literally have all of us on the edge of our seats."

I looked at each of their faces—Jolene's controlled frustration, Magnolia's anxious anticipation, Wrenlee's puzzled concern, Delilah's wide-eyed curiosity, Eliza's amused interest. They were all hanging on my words, waiting for me to reveal the secret that would change everything.

"Mama didn't just leave the house to you, Wrenlee…" I paused for dramatic effect, something I'd learned from watching Magnolia all these years. "She left the house to you for Delilah!!!"

The collective gasp that went up from my family was music to my ears. For a moment, nobody spoke. They just stared at me with their mouths open, processing what I'd just told them.

"What?!" came from multiple voices at once.

Delilah's voice was barely a whisper. "Why would Gran want me to have her house?"

"Oh, for Pete's sake. Let me see the sticky note," Jolene said, reaching for it with hands that trembled slightly.

I handed it over, watching her face as she read aloud: "My gift. Delilah's bed and breakfast."

"She's getting a spin-off!!!!" Eliza exclaimed, and despite everything, I had to laugh. Trust Eliza to find the humor in the moment.

"Mama, what does this mean?" Delilah asked, looking between Wrenlee and the sticky note. "I told Gran years ago that I always wanted to run a bed and breakfast, but I never in a million years thought she took me seriously."

Wrenlee's eyes were soft with understanding. "One thing about your Gran, baby… She always took everything seriously. I guess her last wish was to make one of your dreams come true."

Delilah looked overwhelmed, scared even. "But, I don't want this if it is going to cause a rift between all of you."

I watched Jolene's face as she processed this revelation. The hurt was still there, but it was mixing with something else now—understanding, maybe even relief.

"You know what, baby?" Jolene said slowly. "I think this is the perfect thing for Mama to have done with this old house."

"I absolutely agree," I said, feeling lighter than I had in years. Then, because I couldn't resist, I added with a grin, "You've always wanted to boss people around, now you will get to."

Delilah laughed, but her eyes were still worried. "What about you, Aunt Nolie? I don't want to do this if it is going to cause you any more hurt feelings."

I held my breath, waiting for Magnolia's response. This was the moment that would determine whether Mama's plan would work or if it would just create new wounds.

Magnolia's eyes filled with tears, but they were different tears from the ones she'd been crying all weekend. These looked like hope. "Baby… Could you use a partner?"

"Are you serious?" Delilah's voice shot up an octave.

"You'd want to do that, Magnolia?" Wrenlee asked, and I could hear the surprise in her voice.

"Definitely." Magnolia's voice grew stronger, more certain. "I have felt so lost the last several years. Floating around in the world. Doing my own thing. I never felt like I truly had a purpose. Not until coming back home and spending these last few days with all of you. I know we've had our ups and downs, but I haven't truly felt home until I walked through that door the other day. Wyatt is grown. My lease is up at the end of the month. There is nothing keeping me away from being here."

Delilah launched herself across the room and into Magnolia's arms, and I felt tears prick at my own eyes. This was what Mama had seen, wasn't it? This was what she'd known would happen if she just gave us the right push.

"What about your job?" Jolene asked, ever practical.

Magnolia grinned sheepishly. "Well…"

"Uh oh. Story time!" Eliza interjected, and we all laughed.

"I quit before I came here."

"What? Why?" Jolene looked shocked.

"They didn't want to let me have the time off, and I needed to be here. I am done running away. I have enough money in my savings account to last me several months. I'm here and don't plan on going anywhere."

"You can stay in the house until we can get it up and running and find you somewhere to live," Delilah offered.

"I was hoping you'd say that."

Wrenlee's maternal instincts kicked in. "Well, what about you, baby? I know you are an adult, but you are still my little girl. Are you sure you want to do this?"

"I do. And I want you to do it with me."

"Now, Delilah, you know I can't do that."

"Why not? What is keeping you in California? Your job? I'm sure you can find a teaching job here for next year. Or at least until we get this place going and you can handle the breakfast for the bed and breakfast. You know toasters are my only skillset in the kitchen."

I watched Wrenlee's face as she wrestled with the decision. She'd built a life in California, but I could see the longing in her eyes. The pull of family, of home, of being part of something bigger than herself.

"I would love to do this with you, baby. You know I will always support you in any way that I possibly can."

"I know you will. You always have. So, let's do it!!"

"Okay! I'm in! Let's do it."

The energy in the room was electric now, all of us caught up in the excitement of this new possibility. But Jolene was still looking thoughtful, and I could practically see the wheels turning in her head.

"You know? Your uncle Bobby has loved fishing ever since he retired. He was sad when I told him he couldn't come with me this weekend."

"What're you saying?" Delilah asked.

"Do you think you have a place for a seasoned accountant on your staff?"

"You??" Delilah's voice was pure delight.

"Only if you want me! You won't hurt my feelings."

"You think Bobby would be okay with moving here?" Magnolia asked.

"He has mentioned it several times to be closer to Mama. Though we didn't do it then, now seems as good a time as any."

"Yes! Please!"

I sat back on the couch, watching my family come together around this shared dream, and felt a contentment I hadn't experienced in years. This was what Mama had planned all along, wasn't it? Not to divide us, but to unite us. Not to hurt us, but to heal us.

"Well, it seems like things are really shaping up for y'all," I said. "I'm so glad no one is angry or hurt anymore."

Delilah turned to me with a mischievous glint in her eye. "Aunt Merr, you don't happen to know any awesome event planners, do you? I think it would be fun to have some themed events throughout the year!"

My heart leaped. "Well, let me see, I'm sure I know of someone… ME! Me. Choose me!"

"I was hoping you'd say that. And you already live close by."

"Yep. I can be here anytime."

This was it. This was what I'd been waiting for my whole life without even knowing it. Not just to be included, but to be essential. To have something that was mine to contribute, skills that were needed and valued.

"There is only one stipulation I have for this," Delilah said, her voice growing serious. "If we are going to do it. We will be equal partners. Split it six ways."

"That is so generous. But six? Who is the sixth?" Jolene asked.

Delilah looked at Eliza with obvious affection. "Have y'all not seen how well Eliza takes care of all of us? She can also fold fitted sheets. I mean, who is able to do that? That is, Eliza.. If you want to?"

Eliza's face crumpled with emotion. "I would LOVE to! I don't know what it is about you ladies, but I have truly enjoyed my time here with you the past few days. I've never had a family of my own, and you all welcomed me into yours with wide-open arms."

"We love you, Eliza. You are family," Wrenlee said, and I nodded along with everyone else. It was true. Somehow, over the course of this difficult weekend, Eliza had become one of us.

"So, are we really going to do this? Together?" Delilah asked, looking around at all of us.

"All in favor say Aye!" Eliza called out.

"Aye!!!" we all shouted in unison, and the sound echoed through the house like a promise, like a vow, like the beginning of something beautiful.

"Then, so be it," Delilah said solemnly.

Magnolia shook her head with rueful affection. "Ugh, Mama. You stinker. You really had us all in an uproar for nothing."

"I bet her and your Daddy are getting a real good kick out of this right now," Eliza said.

"I know they are," Jolene agreed.

"So, what are we going to call it?" Wrenlee asked.

"The bed and breakfast?" I clarified.

"Yes."

"It needs to be bold. Something people will remember," Magnolia said, her marketing mind already kicking into gear.

"I have an idea, if that is okay?" Eliza offered hesitantly.

"We are all partners now. Your ideas are always okay," Delilah assured her.

"We all know Breakfast at Tiffany's… What about Breakfast at Delilah's?"

"Oooo, I love that," Magnolia said immediately.

"And it could just be Delilah's for short!" I added, caught up in the excitement.

"Breakfast at Delilah's…" Delilah repeated thoughtfully, testing how it sounded.

"What do you think, baby?" Wrenlee asked.

"I love it! As long as y'all are okay with it being my name on it."

"It's your house, honey. You're just taking us all along for the ride," Jolene said with a warmth I hadn't heard from her in years.

"Absolutely. I think Breakfast at Delilah's is stunningly perfect," Magnolia agreed.

Delilah looked around at all of us, her eyes shining with tears of joy. "I really love you all. Hey, Gran? Thank you for this. I hope that I make you proud."

"You already do, baby," Wrenlee said softly.

I leaned back on the couch—my couch, in my family's house, surrounded by the people I loved most in the world—and marveled at how completely everything had changed in the space of a few hours. This morning, we'd been four broken women fighting over scraps of our mother's love. Now we were partners, dreamers, a family united by purpose and possibility.

Mama had done it again. Even in death, she'd found a way to give us exactly what we needed, even when we didn't know we needed it. The house had never been about the house at all. It had been about bringing us home to each other.

And for the first time in my life, I hadn't just been along for the ride. I'd been the one to reveal the destination. I'd been the one with the answer, the solution, the key to everything.

Finally, finally, it had been my moment. And it was perfect.

20

What She Left Behind

-Delilah-

Six Months Later - Saturday Morning

The smell of fresh coffee and cinnamon rolls fills every corner of what used to be Gran's house. Now it's something entirely new—Breakfast at Delilah's—and somehow, it feels more like home than it ever did before.

I stand in the kitchen doorway, watching Mama flip pancakes while Aunt Nolie arranges fresh flowers in mason jars for the table. Through the window, I can see Aunt Jolene showing Uncle Bobby how to properly set up the fishing equipment for our guests, and Aunt Merr is out front hanging the new sign that arrived yesterday. Eliza is somewhere upstairs, probably making beds with those impossible hospital corners she's somehow mastered.

Six months. It's been six months since that Sunday afternoon when everything changed, when Gran's final surprise turned our family upside down and somehow set us right side up all at once.

We spend so much time rushing, don't we? Rushing to grow up, to move out, to get away. I think about all the years I spent wanting to be anywhere but here, wanting to be older, more independent, more sophisticated than small-town life could offer. I was so busy looking ahead that I almost missed what was right in front of me.

We get busy. We get tired. We get annoyed. Lord knows our family has perfected the art of getting on each other's nerves. Just last week, Aunt Nolie and Aunt Jolene had a twenty-minute argument about whether the guest bathroom should have lavender or eucalyptus soap. The week before that, Mama and I disagreed about the breakfast menu so intensely that Uncle Bobby had to play mediator. And don't get me started on Aunt Mer's very strong opinions about event lighting.

But here's the thing I've learned: families aren't supposed to be easy. They're supposed to be real.

We think we'll call tomorrow. Visit next week. Fix things next time. That's what I used to tell myself whenever I'd think about calling Gran. Tomorrow I'll have more time. Next week won't be so busy. Next month I'll visit for longer. But time doesn't wait for our good intentions, does it? Time moves forward whether we're ready or not, whether we've said the things we need to say or not.

What if next time never comes?

That thought used to terrify me. In those first weeks after Gran died, I'd lie awake thinking about all the conversations we never had, all the questions I never asked.

What was she like when she was my age? What did she dream about? What were her thoughts on social media and smartphones and all the ways the world has changed?

But then I realized something. Next time did come. Just not in the way I expected.

What if all you're left with are boxes? Boxes full of things that don't seem important—until they're all you have left.

We found so many boxes in this house. Boxes of photographs and letters, old recipes written in Gran's careful handwriting, programs from high school plays that Mama and my aunts were in, report cards and birthday cards and Christmas ornaments that looked like they'd been made by children's hands decades ago.

At first, those boxes felt overwhelming. How do you sort through an entire life? How do you decide what to keep and what to let go? But as we worked through them together—Mama and my aunts taking turns sharing stories, laughing over old photographs, sometimes crying over memories that felt too precious to put away—I realized we weren't just sorting through things. We were sorting through ourselves.

See, the funny thing about family is… they drive you crazy. They push your buttons. They bring up things you thought you buried ten years ago.

Trust me, I know. Living with all of them these past six months has been an education in patience I never asked for. Aunt Nolie still leaves her coffee cups everywhere. Aunt

Jolene still tries to manage everyone's schedule. Aunt Merr still hoards craft supplies like the world might run out of glitter. And Mama still worries about everything and everyone to an almost comical degree.

But they're also the only people who knew you when you were still figuring out who you are.

They remember stories about me that I'd completely forgotten. Like the time I was seven and insisted on wearing my Halloween costume to the grocery store in January because I'd decided I was a professional princess. Or when I was twelve and wrote a ten-page business plan for a lemonade stand that was going to "revolutionize the beverage industry." Or when I was fifteen and thought I knew everything about everything and announced that I was never getting married because love was "statistically improbable."

They hold your history. And if you're lucky… they help you carry it.

That's what we've been doing, isn't it? Carrying each other's histories, sharing the weight of memory and love and loss. When Aunt Nolie has days when she misses her old life and wonders if she made the right choice, we remind her of all the ways she's made this place beautiful. When Aunt Jolene gets overwhelmed by the business side of things, we remind her that her organizational skills are what keep us all from drowning in chaos. When Aunt Merr doubts whether her event ideas are too much, we remind her that "too much" is exactly what makes our guests feel special.

And when I have moments—and I do have them—when I wonder if I'm too young, too inexperienced, too naive to be running a business, they remind me that every great dream starts with someone brave enough to believe it's possible.

So if there's one thing I hope you take from all of this—from our story, from our mess, from our perfectly imperfect family—it's this:

Call your people.

Not tomorrow. Not next week. Today. Right now. Call them and tell them you love them. Call them and ask about their day. Call them and share something silly or important or completely mundane. It doesn't matter what you say—what matters is that you say something.

Say the thing.

You know what I mean. That apology you've been putting off. That "I love you" that feels too vulnerable. That "I'm proud of you" or "I miss you" or "I was wrong." Whatever it is that's been sitting in your heart, waiting for the right moment—say it. Because the right moment is now. The right moment is always now.

Apologize first.

Pride is overrated. I've watched my family spend years dancing around hurt feelings and old grudges, each waiting for the other to make the first move. But you know what? Life's too short to wait for someone else to be brave first. Be the one who extends the olive branch. Be the one who says "I'm sorry" even when you're not sure you're entirely wrong. Be the one who chooses love over being right.

Laugh loud.

Fill your house with noise and joy and the kind of laughter that makes your stomach hurt. We do that here now—we laugh at Eliza's terrible jokes and Uncle Bobby's fishing stories and the way Aunt Merr gets so excited about party planning that she starts speaking in run-on sentences. We laugh at ourselves when things go wrong, which they do, regularly, because we're six strong-willed people trying to run a business together.

Hug longer than you think you should.

This one might be the most important. We've become a family of huggers here at Breakfast at Delilah's. Guests comment on it all the time—how we hug each other goodbye every evening, how we hug hello every morning, how we hug for no reason at all other than that we're grateful to be together. Those hugs saved us, I think. They bridged the gaps that words couldn't reach.

Because in the end, the only thing that really matters… is love.

Not money, though we need enough to keep the lights on. Not success, though we're grateful when our guests leave happy reviews. Not perfection, though we strive to do our best every day.

Love. Messy, stubborn, perfectly imperfect love.

The kind of love that forgives when someone eats the last piece of bacon that was supposed to be for a guest's breakfast. The kind of love that shows up at 5 AM to help prep when someone's feeling under the weather. The kind of love that holds you when you cry over a bad day and celebrates with you when something wonderful happens.

The kind of love that says "I choose you" every single day, even when—especially when—you're being difficult.

That's what lasts.

Not the arguments or the hurt feelings or the moments when we wanted to strangle each other. Those fade. But love? Love grows stronger. Love deepens. Love finds new ways to express itself, like turning a grieving family into business partners, like transforming an old house into a place where strangers become friends over shared meals.

That's what we keep.

The memories and the laughter and the way Mama's face lights up when a guest compliments her biscuits. The way Aunt Nolie hums while she arranges flowers. The way Aunt Jolene's eyes crinkle when she's truly happy. The way Aunt Merr bounces on her toes when she's excited about a new event idea. The way Eliza makes everyone feel like they're her favorite person in the world.

That's what we pass on.

Not just recipes and family stories, though those matter too. But the understanding that family isn't just who you're born to—it's who you choose to love, day after day, in small ways and big ways and all the ways in between.

I can hear them now, my chosen family, my inherited family, my perfectly imperfect family. Mama's calling for help with the breakfast rush. Aunt Nolie's laughing at something Eliza said. Aunt Jolene's giving Uncle Bobby detailed instructions about something he probably already knows how to do. Aunt Merr's phone is ringing—probably another client who wants to book our event space.

This is our life now. Busy and chaotic and filled with the kind of love that doesn't always look pretty but always, always feels like home.

Gran knew what she was doing, giving us this gift. Not just the house—though Lord knows we're grateful for it—but the reason to come together, to stay together, to build something beautiful out of the pieces of what we thought we'd lost.

She gave us each other. She gave us purpose. She gave us a second chance to get it right.

And every morning, when I wake up in this house that holds all our history and all our dreams, I whisper a little thank you to her. For seeing what we couldn't see. For believing what we couldn't believe. For loving us enough to know that sometimes the best gift isn't what you expect—it's what you need.

So here's to love. Here's to family. Here's to second chances and new beginnings and the courage to build something beautiful out of something broken.

Here's to breakfast at Delilah's, where every meal comes with a side of belonging and every guest leaves feeling like family.

Here's to what we keep, what we pass on, what lasts. What she left behind – for all of us.

Here's to love—messy, stubborn, perfectly imperfect love.

Because in the end, that's all we really have.

And it's everything.